Greenwich Mean Time

Greenwich Mean Time

A novelisation by Chris Martin
Based on the screenplay by Simon Mirren

SCREENPRESS BOOKS

First published 1999
by ScreenPress Books
8 Queen Street Southwold Suffolk IP18 6EQ

Typeset by RefineCatch Limited, Bungay, Suffolk
Printed in England by Cox & Wyman Ltd., Reading, Berkshire

Chris Martin is identified as the author of this work in
accordance with Section 77 of the Copyright, Designs and
Patents Act 1988

*This book is sold subject to the condition that it shall not, by way
of trade or otherwise, be lent, resold, hired out or otherwise circulated
without the publisher's prior consent in any form of binding or cover
other than that in which it is published and without a similar condition
including this condition being imposed on the subsequent purchaser*

A CIP record for this book
is available from the British Library

ISBN 1 901680 43 6

For more information on forthcoming ScreenPress Books,
contact the publishers at:

ScreenPress Books
8 Queen Street
Southwold Suffolk
IP18 6EQ

Fax: 01502 725422
or visit our Web Site at www.screenpress.co.uk

10 9 8 7 6 5 4 3 2 1

Contents

Vision – San Fu Maltha
Talent – Simon Mirren
Agent – Jessica Woollard
Connection – Clare Taylor
Cavalry – Jonathan Tilston
Inspiration – Dominic & Sam
Gene pool – Gerry, Frances & Kirsteen

"Only the good get lucky"
CM, 1999

Foreword

Parts of *Greenwich Mean Time* are based on a true story.

On 17 December 1990, in a darkened room in Carlshalton's Intensive Care Unit, a group of friends stood in silence over the broken body of a young man who, at 22, had barely begun his life. We'll call him Charlie.

Charlie, up until that point in his life, had been inseparable from the three men who stood around him. They had met as children. They had shared the crazy days of pubescent life: their first cigarette, their first joint, the sudden loss of their virginity and the day they left school. They had shared the pubs, the fights, the being thrown out of the pubs for the fights and the throwing up together in the car parks of the same pubs. They had taken their first ecstasy pill together and grown up through the raves, the giving-up on college, the job centre, the dole, the girlfriend, the pregnant girlfriend, the broken hearts, the leaving home, the flat and the shock of their first electricity bill. With the Intensive Care Unit came the sudden realisation that they were no longer teenagers; worst of all, the reality that one of them was bolted to a bed and paralysed from the neck down, his life now supported by a multitude of machinery.

I was one of those friends, and I can tell you that all of our lives changed on that day. Like Charlie, we had no idea of what being paralysed would really mean. And when we did, it led us all to look back over the days, years and months that preceded the accident, with reverence and longing.

As Charlie began the slow and painful process of healing, we would visit him as regularly as we could, sometimes together, sometimes alone. His life was on hold at a time when our lives and careers had begun to change irrevocably. Girlfriends became wives and babies soon followed. We were shaping our future, moving on and leaving all that we had been behind us. All he could do was watch and wonder what life would bring him once he left the safe confines of the hospital.

Almost a year to the day after the accident, Charlie was wheeled out of hospital to begin his new life. What happened to him then and the journey that he embarked on thereafter, I could never hope to write; only he could do that. But I do know that it was a long and painful process, and one that will probably never truly end.

As Charlie began his rehabilitation, I started to write *Greenwich Mean Time*. During the day I worked on building sites around London and in the evenings I would type away on an old typewriter. For five years on and off I wrote. The story moving on a little at a time as the days unfolded.

Unlike my friends, I had learnt and achieved little at school. The structure of storytelling in *Greenwich Mean Time* probably proves this. There is no one protagonist, or antagonist. The girls in the story are not paid off as well as they should and deserve to be. But I wanted to tell a story about the friendships that had so shaped my future. The only people I thought would ever read it were those who inspired me to write it. Now it is a book and a film and, for me, the experience of watching hundreds of people make Charlie's experience come to life on the big screen.

Whatever happens to this story, book or film, how it is received or not received, is of no real importance. What is important is that, through all of what happened to Charlie, myself and our friends, we are still strong. Our children now play together, and whatever life brings them, if it brings them the friendship that we have shared, they will fare well.

I believe that all that we are and all that we become is owed to our experiences in life. And for me, some of the best and most informative of my experiences are owed to the best friends I have ever known.

. . . for Jason

Simon Mirren
London 1999

Greenwich Mean Time

The wheel of Charlie's chair sank into a soft lump of peat. With a grunt, Rix pushed it free.

"Far enough?" he asked.

"Yeah." Rix flicked down the brake of Charlie's chair with his toe.

Seagulls crowed above them, swooping low across the shore-line ahead of a rush of strong sea wind. Charlie shivered and pulled the fat collar of his Puffa jacket tight at his throat. "Fuck me, it's cold."

Rix slapped his shoulder.

"Mother nature, mate."

Charlie took a deep breath of the crisp spring air and looked around the tiny bay. Bar a few squat cottages, they were alone with the water. The sharp cut of the silver waves framed beautifully against the warm green bank of the mountains.

"Yeah. This'll do all right."

"You reckon he's gonna show?"

"Maybe," said Charlie. He looked up and down the thin strip of grey Irish sand at his feet. "You know he was born here."

"You're kidding."

"No. Bean had all these picture of him here as a nipper."

There was an angry shout behind them as Rix's girlfriend, Sherry, slid on some wet turf.

"Careful, babe," he shouted. "Don't seem much of a choice, does it? Living here or rotting your life away in some council block."

"Fuck knows where he went wrong."

"Rix!" Sherry screamed again.

"Hang on." Rix caught Sherry as she struggled in the mud. "Let me take her," he said as he lifted the child out of her arms.

"This is ridiculous." Sherry steadied herself against him.

She cocked her foot and checked the heel of her boot with gloved fingers. "He ain't even going to show."

"He'll show," said Sam.

Sam stood by the boot of his car back near what passed for a track. The others stood beside him, taking it in turns to unload coats and scarves to wrap up against the cold.

"You seem very sure of yourself," said Sherry.

"Sam sure of himself? That's unusual," said Rix, sniggering.

"I'm not being funny," said Sam. "I just know he'll show."

"You all right now?" said Rix, holding Sherry's arm to steady her.

"Yeah."

"Is your beautiful daughter going to be warm enough, Sherry," called Sam.

"She'll be fine."

"And you?"

Sherry stepped forward with a jerk as her heel sank into the earth.

"Just about."

Rix re-joined Charlie at the water's edge. Charlie was checking his watch.

"Nearly twelve."

Rix grunted.

Charlie took a deep breath.

"Don't seem like us somehow, does it?"

"What you do you mean?"

"All this," said Charlie. He rapped the arm of his chair with a knuckle. "And all this."

"Sometimes it's worth it," said Rix.

Charlie turned to face him. Rix was rocking the child in his arms. "Yeah, maybe." Charlie smiled.

"Hey, check it out," called Sam.

Rix and Charlie turned to see a little red hire car making its way down the track which led to the beach.

"Fuck me, he came," said Charlie.

The car bumped off the track and came to a halt next to Sam. A middle-aged man with a ruddy face stepped out of the driver's seat. He wore a threadbare tweed suit and stained black tie.

"Glad you could make it," said Sam. The man nodded. He walked around his car and popped open the boot. Reaching inside it, he lifted out a plain steel casket. He looked grimly around the assembled group and then walked past them and across to the shore.

He paused by the water and looked around the bay.

"Brings back memories," he announced. He dropped his head and sighed. "Right, let's get on with it."

1

THE LAST DAY OF SCHOOL

The big Perspex wall clock was ticking impossibly slowly toward the final five o'clock bell of their schooldays. Each tiny movement of the hands went another step towards drowning out the form teacher's final monologue.

"Right, ladies and gentleman," he said, glancing at the clock. "It seems we are coming to the end of our long and fruitful relationship." The form teacher, Mr Aherene, addressed the class in his regular uniform of cardigan, Hush Puppies and black-frame specs. He paced in front of the battered whiteboard, mucky with a thousand wipings. This afternoon 'Your Future', 'Achievement' and 'Responsibility' had just been written in fat round writing in the centre of it, while 'Aherene is a wanker' had been tattooed for posterity in its bottom right corner with a biro. A goodbye gift from the students.

"Five years ago, I stood here and told you of the journey you were all about to embark on. How some would excel and some would fail. How you would grow up and shape yourselves into adults. How one day you could become the doctors, the sportsmen or, God help us, the politicians of the future."

Mr Aherene paused to clean his lenses on a hanky.

"A few of you are going off into further education and some of you are staying on to join the sixth form."

A groan went up. Mr Aherene raised his voice another octave to make his point.

"But for the rest of you . . ." He fixed them with a gaze over the top of his glasses. ". . . that day has come. You lot are going out into what we call the real world." Mr Aherene picked his dog-eared register off his desk, attempting to give some drama to his speech. "Now, as most of you don't even seem to know what day it is, I'm intrigued to know what you intend to do with the rest of your lives."

He opened the register and nudged his glasses back onto the bridge of his nose.

"I'm going to call out your names one by one and I want you to stand up and tell the class – briefly – what your plans for the future are."

Three scruffy teenage boys sat two rows from the back of the class, crushed into tiny school desks. Rix, Bean and Sam had been best mates since day one. Three cheeky monkeys altogether unsuited to the classroom. Rix – hear no evil – a well-built West Indian with close-cropped dreadlocked hair. A bulbous pair of headphones hung perpetually around his neck. Bean – speak no evil – skinny and awkward, stared blankly back at Mr Aherene as he talked. Sam – see no evil – had the looks of a model and the cotton-wool brain to match. Rich too. His Dad had died and left him a packet. The only one missing from their little posse was Charlie, but then he had always had a problem with punctuality; particularly if it was Mr Aherene's class.

"As Mr Rowntree hasn't bothered to grace us with his presence, Rix, you can start us off."

Rix was busy scratching the back of his head and drumming his fingers on the desk. He screwed his face up painfully as his name was called.

"You always pick on me, Sir."

"It's cause you're *blik*," said Sam. The class erupted.

"Well, Rix?" asked Mr Aherene, rising above the commotion.

Rix stood up heavily from his desk. "Start up a band, make millions of squids."

"Sweet!" said Sam. "You can pay me back that tenner you owe me.

"Shag thousands of birds . . ." continued Rix. " . . . get a *serious* drug habit and I guess O.D. before I'm thirty, Sir." He sat back down again with a sloppy grin; half in triumph and half to shield himself from the hailstorm of rolled-up paper.

"Very commendable. How about learning a skill, a trade?"

"Skill! I am skilled," said Rix, outraged. "I'm a fucking musician."

"Indeed," replied Mr Aherene, checking the register. "How about our social commentator, Sam Jackson."

The class whooped. Sam stood up, with an assured nonchalance.

"Well, as you know, Sir, my kick-boxing career is over." He pointed to his eye. "Damage to the retina; Hong Kong. So, after much thought, I've decided to move to Paris and eke out a living as a gigolo."

"I doubt very much if you can even *spell* gigolo, let alone perform as one," said Mr Aherene. "Still, judging by your performance at this school, I can't see you being able to achieve a lot more than that."

"Oh, come on, Sir, that ain't fair."

"Fair, Mr Jackson? Fair doesn't come into it in the game of life."

Mr Aherene turned his attention to Bean, who was hunched over his desk smirking at Sam. "You seem pretty confident, Mr McCormack. What are you planning for the next fifty years?"

"Well, Sir," started Bean nervously.

"He's going to be a professional wanker, Sir," said a voice from the back of the class. It was Elroy; a real product of the concrete jungle from the same estate as Bean. He'd spent the last five years at the back of the class with his face wrapped round a Game Boy.

"Stand up, Bean," said Mr Aherene. "Come on."

"Yeah, stand up, you prat!" said Elroy, leaning forward to shove Bean on the back.

Sam swung round. "Oi! Leave it out."

"Calm down, gentlemen," said Mr Aherene, "Bean, please carry on."

"I dunno, Sir. Get a job maybe?" said Bean cautiously.

"What about your trumpet?"

Bean shrugged.

"We'll see what happens with the band, Sir."

"Ah, your band." Mr Aherene's eyes lit up. "Mr Johnson tells me you have talent."

"Charlie reckons I should go to music college," Bean blurted.

"And you?"

Bean thought for a second.

"Nah! I get dizzy when I go north of the river," said Bean. The class hooted with laughter.

Charlie Rowntree burst into the classroom, his face flushed from running. A cheer went up in celebration of Charlie's lateness. He held up his thin arms in triumph.

"Perfect timing for the fourth member of the gang. You'll be late for your own funeral, Mr Rowntree," said Mr Aherene.

Charlie wore a heavy Nikon camera around round his neck which he swung under one arm as he swaggered towards his teacher. "Oh, I hope not, Sir," he said with a charming smile.

"I suppose there's no point trying to push you for some kind of explanation for your tardiness?"

"Been to see the nurse, Sir. *Sexual* problem."

"Sit down."

"I've been looking into the possibility of a job, as it happens." Charlie gave a thumbs-up sign to Sam.

"A job?" said Mr Aherene. "With whom, might I ask?"

"British Rail!" called out Sam.

"Yeah, British Rail," said Charlie. "So what's been going on here then?"

"I think it's time you all woke up and joined the real world."

Charlie ignored him, choosing instead to wink across the classroom at his girlfriend, Lucy.

"Well, don't you?"

Charlie flicked his long blond quiff back and fixed Mr Aherene with his clear blue eyes.

"You talking to me?" he said in a heavy New York accent. "You talking to me?"

"*Raging Bull*," called out Rix.

"No, no, *Taxi Driver*," said Mr Aherene wearily.

Charlie slapped five with him. "Hang on," he said taking

7

a step back. He pointed his camera at Mr Aherene. "Could you turn a little to the left, Sir?"

"Your interest in photography is laudable, however now is not the time."

"Oh, come on, Sir, just one last piccy," pleaded Charlie. He twirled the camera's long, black lens to focus the shot. "You know you got a real interesting face."

Mr Aherene put one hand on his hip and gave a camp smile. The shutter clicked.

"Gotcha! I'll make you a star, darling."

Wolf whistles rang round the classroom. The electronic beeping of a digital watch ushered in a rustle of anticipation.

"Hey! Sit back down. Not until the bell!"

"But ye cannae take away our freedom," shouted Rix.

"You had better hope your last few hours of education prove more rewarding than the previous five years, Mr Stanley."

At the back of the class Sam leant over Elroy's desk, casting a shadow across the yellow screen of his Game Boy.

"Oi, fuck off! Can't see nothing."

Sam looked Elroy in the eyes, his face was a mask of dramatic intent.

"I've seen things you little people wouldn't believe. Attack ships on fire off the shoulder of Orion, bright as magnesium . . . I rode on the back decks of a blinker and watched C-beams glitter in the dark near the Tannhauser Gate. All those moments lost, like tears in rain."

"*Bladerunner*," shouted Bean.

Charlie slapped him on the back.

"Time to die." Sam swung his fingers up clasped like a gun. He mimed firing three heavy-calibre shots into Elroy's chest. Elroy shoved his desk into Sam's knees.

"Fuck your mamma, rich boy." He stood up and glared at Sam.

"Whooooo," said Sam with a limp-wristed whine.

"You ain't always gonna have some teacher to protect you."

"Hark at her," said Charlie.

The class bell rang and the class descended into a chaos of torn off ties and thrown textbooks.

Charlie grabbed Sam in a headlock and rubbed his knuckles across the top of Sam's head.

"Come on, Son, we've got work to do."

Elroy dropped his head and mumbled to himself in a phoney Jamaican patois: "Batty boys."

They were alone in the railway carriage. Bean, on look-out and stop-watch duty, stood in the aisle and looked nervously from side to side for conductors. Sam was on back-up and already sitting on the steel edge of a push-down window. Half his body was out the window while his legs and feet dangled into the carriage. Rix was the anchorman. He knelt on the grubby floor of the train among the fag butts and empty crisp packets. He held Sam's legs in a one-handed embrace to stop him falling out the window. With the other he tried vainly to brush the dusty marks Sam's shoes made off his trousers.

"Come on, man, this is fucking crazy," said Bean

"Just watch the time," said Rix, looking up at Sam. "All right, man?" Sam nodded.

Outside he gave Charlie's legs one final shove. Just enough to slide his friend onto the roof of the train. Charlie scrambled upright and swivelled his body against the blast of wind which whipped across the grey steel of the train's curved roof.

"Okay," shouted Charlie. His squinted into the wind and tried to make out the familiar red walls of the B&Q warehouse.

Sam waved and then bent double to peer into the carriage. "B&Q coming up. You keep an eye on that fucking watch, Bean."

Bean pulled a heavy plastic sports watch out of his trouser pocket. He stabbed at the buttons to reset its stop-watch mode. He looked up nervously.

"Sherry!" he pleaded.

Sherry ran her fingers through her jet-black straightened hair and shook her head. She sat with Lucy on the bank of seats, next to her puffing boyfriend, crouched on the floor in front of them. Sherry ground away at her long colourful nails with a file while Lucy was flicking through a magazine.

"Fucking pricks," she mumbled.

Sherry gave Rix a little kick and went back to filling her nails.

"Do you think you're going to miss school?" said Lucy, looking up from her magazine.

"I doubt it," said Sherry. "Oh, they're nice." She pointed at a pair of shoes in the magazine.

"I think I will."

"Come on, Lucy," said Sherry. "You're off to college. It'll be miles better."

"I suppose. It's just such a big change."

"Yeah, well at least you won't have to put up with this macho bullshit." She poked Rix with her nailfile.

"All right, lover?"

"Sherry, please!"

Bean focused on the view out the window. His eye caught a flash of red livery through the scrubby bushes that lined the track. The B&Q warehouse. From here there was exactly one minute until the tunnel.

"Go!" he shouted and clicked down on the watch to start it.

"Go, Sam," shouted Rix. He flinched with exertion as Sam leaned back out the window.

"Go, Charlie. Go, you mad bastard!"

Charlie pulled his legs up under him, crouching like a sprinter on the blocks. He pulled his Nikon around his belly so it hung from his neck. Slowly he raised himself up from a crouch and smiled as the wind pulled at his cheeks. His blazer spread out behind him like a cape, his school tie flailed like a whip at his throat twisting through his blond hair with the force of the wind. He flung his arms in the air.

"Top of the fucking world, mate."

His heart was beating so hard he could barely catch his breath. His hands found the heavy Nikon and brought the viewfinder up to eye level. Through its tiny window he looked along the length of the train. The great grey tube stretched out along the track in front of him dotted with little mushroom-shaped air vents. Charlie stood astride its apex with his legs spread for stability. On either side of him the boxy gardens and dirty houses of Essex sped past in a green blur punctured with washing lines and discarded children's toys.

"Yes!" he shouted as he shot off a picture. His thumb worked the handle, winding on the film after each shot. Above the rush of the wind he heard Sam calling to him.

"Charlie. Charlie, mate. Forty seconds!" Charlie swung his lens round to look over the edge of the train roof. The railway sleepers that lined the track strobed through the frame like the edge of a roulette wheel. Then Sam's head and torso appeared sticking horizontally out from the side of the train. Sam swung his school blazer round and round his head in slow lazy circles.

"Yeeee . . . Ha!" he cried, whooping like a wrangler. "Come on, you cunts! No more fucking school." He flung the blazer away. Charlie followed the heavy black shape of the blazer as it filled with wind and rose into the air like a great black crow.

The body of the train turned heavily under his feet, the segment of the carriages chasing each other around a sharp corner. Charlie staggered and regained his balance only to see the tunnel coming up ahead. A black mouth sucking the train in like a string of dirty pasta. Hunching himself over and, winding deliberately with his thumb, he prepared himself for one last shot.

"This is going to be the bollocks," he whispered.

Inside the carriage, Bean paced down the aisle between the seats like an expectant father.

"Oh fuck, oh fuck!" he muttered, breaking into a sweat. He held the sports watch tightly in one hand, its strap curled over his fingers. His forehead was lined with worry. "Rix. He's not going to make it." Rix hugged Sam's legs tightly against the raging wind outside.

"How long?" Rix said.

"Twenty seconds."

Rix tilted his head back to shout up through the open window.

"Twenty seconds, Sam."

11

Bean wrenched open a window on the other side of the carriage. He leant out and shouted, "Charlie! Fifteen seconds!"

The tunnel was coming up fast. A hard square of Victorian brick stained with decades of coal smoke, it was a tight fit with only a foot clear on either side. Charlie framed the red-brick arch and began to take a series of shots. The grey metal walkway of the train's roof was disappearing fast.

Bean, his head out the window, could see the sharp edge of the tunnel wall ahead.

"Charlie, for fuck's sake," he shouted. The wall was so close he could read the graffiti on it. He ducked his head sharply back as the whole carriage went black. The roar of the wheels on the track was deafening. Wall lights flickered weakly. Then it was gone. The tunnel disappeared with ear-popping suddenness and the carriage was filled once again with bright sunlight.

"Fuck!" shouted Bean. "Fuck!"

"Great fucking pictures," said Charlie breathlessly behind him. Bean spun round to see him climbing back in through the window. Sam, still half in and half out of the carriage, pressed his face up against the window and blew out his cheeks against the glass like a pasty goldfish. Charlie was wind-swept and exhilarated, covered from head to toe in dirt and smog from the roof of the train. His camera still hung round his neck. Lucy squealed with delight, dropped her magazine and hugged him.

"You are one mad fucking bastard, Charlie boy," she said.

"The maddest," said Charlie as he kissed her.

Rix collapsed back onto his backside, exhausted. He looked up with a sigh and caught Sherry's eye. She shook her head slowly; she was deeply unimpressed.

"Thought you was meant to be watching the time, Bean," said Sam as he followed Charlie through the window.

Charlie was beaming from ear to ear. His dirty shirt was rumpled where Sam had grabbed hold of him at the last minute.

"Yeah, well, I could have done another roll of film easy."

Sam shaped the fingers of his free hand into a circle and made the universal symbol of a wanker.

Greenwich Park was the place for a lazy afternoon with your whole life ahead of you. A long, wide slope of grass that ran right up to the blue dome of the Observatory. Every summer all the local kids went up there to chill out, have a smoke and take in the view. On a clear day you could see right across the river and all the way to Hampstead. Save yourself a lot of leg work if you were a tourist. St Paul's, NatWest Tower, Houses of Parliament and Centre Point; you can see the lot with your arse parked on a rug and a spliff in your hand. Lying there looking down over it all, you feel like you could lean forward and float across the whole city.

"Down there, my fabulous, furry friends, is where Aherene tells us the 'real world' begins." Charlie cast his arm majestic-ally over the London skyline. "We must walk amongst these *Normal Ones* and learn their ways . . . discover our purpose, justify our lives. Then, and only then, will we be truly fulfilled . . . What say you, brothers and sisters? Shall we go forth?"

A football sailed across the afternoon sky and bounced off the back of Charlie's head. "Oi, fuck off!"

"Charlie," said Rix, his arm still raised from the throw, "you *are* a cunt."

Charlie rubbed the back of his head and picked up the ball. "I'm fucking wasted on you cunts."

"You're just wasted, mate," said Rix, laughing. "C'mon. Over here."

Charlie dropped the ball onto his foot, tapped it up in the air a couple of times and then caught it on one knee. He knocked it from knee to knee with perfect control and whis-tled a little tune to himself.

"Don't get flash, Charlie," said Sam.

"Ain't flash," said Charlie as he attempted a particularly flash move. The ball spun up into the air and across the grass towards Sam.

"This is for the record, right?" said Sam, catching the ball on his foot.

The boys, now divested of most of their school uniform, formed a circle to kick the ball between them, trying to keep it in the air for as long as possible.

"One," they said together.

Lucy and Sherry, completely uninterested, sat a few yards away on a tartan rug. Lucy was checking through a big bag of assorted mix for a big ghetto blaster adorned with ganja leaf stickers. Sherry was sitting next to her, making her way though a pile of magazines. Coca-Cola cans and crisp packets were scattered around them.

Sam kicked the ball towards Rix, whose face was tight with concentration.

"Nineteen . . ." Rix bounced the ball briefly on the top of his ankle, returning it to Charlie, who was still being flash

"Twenty! Twenty-one!"

"He truly is a natural . . ." Charlie panted. "This young lad from SE10. What a talent."

He returned the ball to Sam. The ball fell short. Sam, nearly losing it, slid forwards in a painful-looking half-splits, just getting a toe to it.

"Fuck!"

The ball went high but safely back to Charlie.

"Jelly legs!" he said as caught it on his chest and started flicking it from foot to foot. "Twenty-one . . . two . . .! This could be a new record." Back to Sam, who caught it on a more dignified knee

"To you, Bean. Don't fuck this up." Sam turned quickly to Charlie. "Maybe I should take his turn?"

"No man. Rules is fucking rules."

"Thirty-nine . . . Forty . . . You ready, Bean?"

"Yeah." Sam kicked him the ball. He flailed wildly but still managed to get under it. Then he began an uncoordinated dance of wildly swung limbs. The boys watched in horror as Bean followed the ball across the park in a desperate attempt to keep it aloft.

"Forty-one, two . . ."

Bean settled into a rhythm of hopping forward on his left foot and tapping the ball with his right.

"Forty-three. Forty-four. One more, Bean!" shouted Charlie.

The ball hit the ground with a soft, dull thud.

"Wanker!" screamed Sam, throwing his hands in the air. "YOU FUCKING WANKER! We could've broken our record."

"Piss off, Sam. It's only a game, mate," said Charlie.

"Fuck did you say to me?" said Sam, turning on him.

He walked up to Charlie, puffing out his chest and pressing right up to him in mock aggression. Charlie drew himself up to his full height and looked Sam right in the eye.

"You're a big man, but you're out of shape. For me, it's a full-time job. Now behave!"

"*Get Carter*. Right?" said Rix.

"Oh yeah?" said Sam, still holding Charlie's gaze.

"Yeah," said Charlie.

Sam jumped on him. They tumbled to the ground laughing and began to wrestle.

Bean picked up the dropped ball from where it sat at his feet and walked solemnly over to the girls.

"Mind if I . . ." he asked

"Don't worry, Bean," said Lucy. "Come and sit down."

"They're so immature," added Sherry.

Rix came bounding over.

"This is wicked," he said, hearing a song come on the tape player. A mix of house music cut to a heavy dub base line. He turned the volume on the ghetto blaster right up and began to dance. "Come on, Bean, make yourself useful and skin up."

Charlie and Sam joined the group. Sam dragged Charlie behind him in a headlock, their white shirts stained with mud and grass. They stopped a few feet from the others. Charlie popped free and nudged Sam in the ribs with his elbow.

"See that bird there?" he said and pointed at Lucy. "Five times blond baby. Gonna have her."

Lucy giggled.

"No fucking chance, mate," said Sam. "It's me she's after."

"Oh no, mate, she wants me," replied Charlie with a knowing smile. "She just don't know it yet."

"In your dreams," said Lucy.

Charlie performed a running dive onto her wriggling body, smothering her with slobbery kisses. Lucy fought him off, scrabbled up from the rug and ran down the hill with Charlie in hot pursuit.

"You can't fight your feelings," he called after her.

Sam sat down heavily next to Bean, who was busy with rolling papers, tobacco and a bag of grass.

"No offence, mate," said Sam. "Heat of the moment, yeah?"

"Guess so," said Bean.

Rix was wrapped up in his dancing and didn't notice Sherry looking at him, propped up on one elbow on the rug.

"Rix," she said, tugging at his trouser leg. Disturbed, from the rhythms of the music Rix looked down at her.

"Yeah?"

"Let's do it."

"Eh?"

"C'mon, let's do it." Her voice was husky and provocative.

"What? Where?"

"In the bushes."

Rix flushed. "Sherry!" He was shocked.

Bean was nearly finished with the joint. He stuck it in his mouth and fumbled through his pockets for a box of matches. Sam pulled out a blue plastic lighter and lit it for him.

"Soon as we get the demo together, things'll start to happen," said Bean "Then I'm going to America. Visit New York. Los Angeles!" He took a drag and then handed the joint to Sam. "You've been there, ain't you?"

"Only when I was a nipper," said Sam.

"The Grand Canyon. Injun country. Wouldn't you like to go?" said Bean.

"Sure would, partner." He paused. "You've got big dreams, Bean, my boy. Looks like this band of your is going to need a decent manager."

"Eh?" Bean looked worried.

The sound of approaching giggling announced Lucy's return with Charlie still behind her. They collapsed onto the rug. Charlie grabbed her and they rubbed noses, Eskimo style.

"You're a very naughty girl," he said.

"Oooh, vicar," replied Lucy from under him.

"Hello, what's this?" said Rix from his vantage point. He stopped dancing.

"Hello, hello, hello," said Sam.

Fifty yards down the slope in front of them, a group of three girls were setting up camp. Two of them unpacked books and water bottles while the third pulled an acoustic guitar from a plastic case.

"She's a musician," said Bean.

"The man's a mind-reader," said Rix.

Bean smiled.

"I've seen her before at orchestra."

The girl was barefoot. She had striking good looks and curly corkscrew hair which she wore loose over the familiar Thomas Tallis school uniform.

"You been holding out on us, Bean," said Lucy.

Bean blushed.

"Something about a girl in uniform, know what I mean?" said Sam.

The girl strummed a few chords. She looked up and saw Bean scrutinising her. She gave a cheeky grin and returned to her playing. Bean flushed a deep red and looked down quickly at the ground. Rix gave a little wolf whistle.

"Hello, Bean," he said.

"I think you're in there, mate," said Sam.

He passed the joint over Sherry and up to Rix. Rix stuck it between the fingers of his cupped hands so the tip stuck out like a little paper chimney. He took a massive toke and blew a big cloud of smoke above his head.

"Leave it out, Sam," said Sherry. "Why don't you go over and say hello, Bean."

"No, no. I couldn't."

"Oh, come on, Bean. Who dares wins, eh?" said Sherry, putting her arm round him.

"Oh, all right," he said. He didn't need much encouragement. He stood up and stretched the numbness out of his legs.

17

He turned round to check his friends. They flapped him towards her with their hands. "Are you sure?"

"Just go," chorused Sherry and Lucy.

Bean strode down the hill.

"There are three of them," said Charlie. He started to get up. "Perhaps I ought to . . ."

"No, you don't," said Lucy. She grabbed him by the shirt tail and pulled him back down next to her.

As Bean approached, the girl with the guitar stopped playing and looked up at him. Her friends stopped reading and peered over their books. Bean's felt his confidence evaporate under their gaze.

"Hello," said the girl. "Don't I know you from somewhere?"

"Er . . . yeah, maybe, I . . ." Bean's mind went blank. "That's great music you're playing. I'm a musician, er . . . too."

"You're Bean, aren't you? I've seen you in the orchestra. I'm Bobby. This is Karen and Jackie."

"Hello," the two girls said in deadpan voices. Then went back to their books.

"You write that song yourself?" asked Bean.

"Yeah," said Bobby. "You like it?"

"Yeah, it's cool," said Bean, feeling a little more at ease. "I write songs too. I'm in a band with Rix." He pointed up the hill at Rix, who was still standing next to the ghetto blaster with the joint in his hand. He waved.

"I'd like to hear them," said Bobby.

"Cool," said Bean, unable to believe his luck. "Er, I'll make you a tape, if you like."

"Is this man bothering you?" Sam had appeared behind Bean.

"No, he's just offered to make me tape actually," said Bobby.

Bean's heart sank.

"Bean's classic love songs, volume one," said Sam. "*Like a Virgin, Sweet Sixteen and Never Been Kissed, Puppy Love . . .*"

Bean felt a sickly rush of embarrassment in his stomach.

"You don't know shit!" he blurted.

"Who've you gone with then, Casanova?" said Sam cruelly. "Name them . . ."

"No one you know!" snapped Bean.

"I know everyone you fucking know."

"Listen to King Dick over there. He'd suck it himself if it were big enough!" said Bobby.

Her friends laughed.

"Oh, I do, girls. Every night. And I swallow," said Sam.

The girls groaned in disgust. Bobby jumped up.

"C'mon, Bean, don't listen to that prick," she said. "I'll buy you an ice cream. Anyone else want one?"

"Yeah," said Bobby's friends.

"I wouldn't mind either," said Sam.

"I'm sure you know where the van is," said Bobby. "C'mon, Bean."

Sam, left standing, decided to make the best of a bad situation.

"He makes me laugh," he said as Bobby and Bean walked away. "Well, ladies. Fancy a smoke?"

Bean and Bobby walked together down the concrete path that led to the gates of the park. A battered ice cream van spent its summer there, all peeling paint and saggy-looking tyres. The legend *Mr Whippy* had been written in curly writing down one side. The man who sat inside didn't look particularly whippy. He stared aimlessly at a copy of the *Sun* laid out on the counter, struggling with the crossword. A couple of children stood next to the van with their parents. The parents were carrying the footballs, picnic hampers and assorted toys of a day in the park. The children struggled to eat their ice creams without too much of it dribbling onto their hands.

"What you want?" asked Bobby, taking a five-pound note out of the top pocket of her shirt.

"Mint Choc Chip."

"Very exotic."

"Like it almost more than Miles Davis."

"But not quite."

"Not quite."

19

"Two mint choc chip and two vanilla, please."

"Jazz fan, eh?"

"Trumpet innit? He's a genius."

The sour-faced man handed their ice creams through the hatch of the van without a word. He took Bobby's money and rummaged in an old plastic carton for her change.

"Giss a lick," said a voice behind them.

Bean turned to see Elroy. He'd already ditched his school uniform in favour of super-baggy jeans, expensive air filled trainers and a sports top. It looked like someone had already had a crude go at giving him a *home boy* haircut by shaving a line in his close-cropped scalp.

"Elroy, how you doing?"

"So this is where you hang out these days." Elroy was with another black kid from the estate whom Bean didn't recognise. Elroy spoke loudly, addressing his friend as much as Bean. "Too much concrete on the Ferrier for you?" Bean smirked. Elroy looked up and down the road before moving in close to Bean. "Like the green, do ya? Then you'll love this, mate." He reached into the pocket of his trousers and pulled out a clear plastic bag; the kind normally used for loose change in the Post Office. He cupped it in his hand to hide the contents from everyone but Bean and Bobby. The bag contained a small ball of grass.

"Nah. Thanks. Gotta get these to the others before they melt . . . later."

"Straight from the 'Dam, you get me?"

"Nah."

Elroy jumped in front of Bean and Bobby.

"Oi! Ain't you gonna introduce us to your new bird? Or do I fucking embarrass you now?" Elroy spoke in an aggressive tone. He turned to Bobby. "Come on, girl, just one lick for your uncle Elroy, eh?"

"Leave it out, Elroy," said Bean weakly.

"She don't mind, do ya, darling?"

As he reached for Bobby's ice cream his hand was violently slapped down. It was Sam, who had decided to get his own ice cream after all and had brought Charlie and Rix along to boot.

"Yes, she does," he said.

"What the fuck are you doing?" sneered Elroy. "Ain't no teacher to look after you now, wanker."

Sam needed little encouragement. He moved in on Elroy straight away, shoving him backwards past Bean and Bobby with the palm of his hand.

"Oh yeah, you fucking want it?" Elroy's mate began to step forward.

"Don't even fucking think about it, mate," said Charlie.

"That's enough!" said the ice cream man, breaking his silence. He leaned out of the hatch of his van. "Fuck off, I'm trying to run a business."

"Sam, leave it out . . ." said Bean, putting an hand on Sam's shoulder.

"Shut it, Bean." Sam shrugged him off. "This cunt's got it coming."

The parents pulled their kids away from the epicentre of the trouble with their free hands. A little girl dropped her ice cream and started to cry.

"Sam the fucking man," spat Elroy.

Rix grabbed Sam in a loose shoulderlock and pulled him back.

"The kids, man," he said, trying to calm the situation down.

"Fucking wanker," hissed Sam.

"Oi! You deaf?" The ice cream man raised his voice. "I'll call the fucking police on the lot of you." He pulled a mobile phone out from under his grubby apron.

"Fucking fool!"

"Fuck off!"

"Sam, old bill!" said Charlie.

A Park Police van had come into view about a hundred yards down the road. Elroy clocked them too. None too keen to be searched and even less to lose his draw, he backed off, his mate in tow. He shouted after them as he went.

"Fucking losers, Bean, fucking losers."

Sam, calm again, was released by Rix.

"Fucking hell," said Rix with a sigh.

"You all right?" said Sam, putting an arm around Bobby.

"Yeah. I guess so. You burned off enough testosterone?"

"Thanks a lot." Bobby smiled.

"All right. Thank you. Very gallant."

"C'mon. Let's go." They turned and start back up the hill to join Bobby's friends.

Bean, now forgotten, stood with a mint choc chip melting in either hand. He stayed motionless as the group dispersed and the lime-green drips of the melting ice cream rolled over his clenched hands. Bean wondered what was going on with the world when one minute he was talking to the girl of his dreams and the next he was a just another prat with sticky hands.

"Shake a leg, Bean," shouted Charlie somewhere in the distance. Bean dropped the ice creams in an old half-oildrum that served as the van's dustbin and slowly made his way after the others.

2

THREE YEARS LATER

Bean felt his back twang as he dropped another two buckets of heavy plaster onto the concrete floor. His face was spotted with hard round dots of plaster. His tatty overalls, once white, were covered with paint smears, earth and roofing dust. He and Rix worked in an empty room on the first floor of a building site. Its windows were just holes in the wall through which you could see great piles of earth and stacks of scaffolding poles. Rix had finally grown his dreads out, he held them back off his face with a red, gold and green woman's scrunchie. He too was half man, half plaster. He stood on a scaffolder's plank suspended between two ladders and smeared the last of the previous load's thick white pap across the red bricks of the wall. On one end of the plank his ghetto blaster played. It's ganja stickers were now faded and peeling. Like Rix and Bean, it was splattered with the rubbish from a dozen building sites.

"Three more should do it," he said over his shoulder.

"You fancy mixing for a while?"

"Sorry, mate, I've got artistic talent to consider. This is my *cistern* fucking chapel. You get me?"

"Brilliant."

Bean picked up a second trowel from the plank and scratched the side of his head with its tip. With a flash of inspiration, he dug into the pocket of his overalls and pulled out his sports watch.

"Shit, we gotta go, Rix."

"Eh?"

"Band practice."

Rix jumped down from the platform and dropped his trowel into one of the full buckets of plaster that Bean had brought in.

"You ain't going nowhere till this room's fucking done," said a harsh voice from the door. Brian, Bean's dad, stood on the threshold. He was also dressed in the filthy overalls but wore a faded tweed jacket over the top for warmth. He held a rolled copy of the *Daily Express* like a baton in one fist. A thin roll-up cigarette hung from his lips.

"But, Dad, you promised . . ."

"But, Dad, you promised," he mimicked. "I promised fuck all, now shut it and get a fucking move on." Bean stared at him with burning resentment. "You want to wank over that fucking trumpet with your mates, you do it when I ain't paying you. You got that?" Brian turned and walked out.

Bean threw his trowel against the freshly plastered wall. It dug a long thin scar in the soft plaster before clattering onto the concrete floor.

"That ain't gonna help nothing, mate," said Rix. "Get mixing, we're gonna be late."

The DHSS office reminded Sam of a converted gents' toilet. The walls were painted in a dull battleship grey, the floor was a grainy concrete dotted with discarded cigarette ends and sweet wrappers. The walls were decorated with posters advertising the latest government initiatives, which invariably featured men in overalls or chef's hats giving the thumbs-up to the camera. The posters went a long way towards convincing Sam that he should never nine to five it for a living. Along one wall was a bleak row of plastic chairs. Few people stayed there long enough to sit on them. Those who did normally had trouble with their claims and stood to miss a whole week's money. They'd sit, chain-smoking cigarettes angrily, their eyes wide open for any sign of activity from the office. The other side of the room was entirely taken up with a row of Plexiglass booths which would have been more at home in a bank. Above each window a letter of the alphabet had been stencilled. As almost all of the booths were shut, covered from the inside with blinds, whatever system the council had once hoped would operate here had long since broken down. The two booths which were open were manned by surly council employees dressed with a half-hearted attempt at authority in business suits. They looked just as bored as those who stood in the straggling queues. A burly, black security guard stood by the door to deal with those who were too drunk or too angry to wait calmly.

As Sam entered he took off his Ray-Bans and tucked them into the top pocket of his Ben Sherman shirt. He brushed down the creases of his Staypress trousers without thinking. Somewhere in the back of his mind he thought he might pick up some of the dirt and failure from the office. Whatever the risks, it was still free money and that was something even Sam was not too big for. He took his place in the queue behind a ruddy-looking man who wore wellington boots and a woollen hat despite the summer heat.

When Sam reached the front of the queue he slid his UB40 card through the grille and received a piece of paper back to sign. A gnawed plastic biro had been sellotaped to a limp spring by the booth for just such a purpose. Sam didn't like to touch it. Instead he pulled a gold Parker pen from his pocket. He signed the form flamboyantly before picking up his UB40 and turning to go.

"Wait a minute," said the woman in the booth. She was squinting at the monitor on her desk "You got *Restart* next week."

"*Restart* for what?" said Sam.

"Work! You know, like what I do."

"You work?"

The woman from the dole office did not seem amused.

"Do the *Restart*, or look for a job, or no money. It's that simple."

"It's just not going to be convenient, I'm afraid."

"Mr Jackson, your *Restart* has already been cancelled several times." The woman tapped at her keyboard. "A family bereavement, some sort of debilitating illness for which no doctor's letter was subsequently provided, community work – again unconfirmed . . ."

"Just so happens I got a week's work. I was gonna claim for

it, so if you could arrange the *Restart* for another time . . ."

The woman in the booth paused and looked at Sam, who had raised his eyebrows in a gesture of sincerity.

"Oh, all right. But this really is the last time we can . . ."

"Thanks. And may I say I love what you've done with the hair."

"We do this for your benefit, you know."

"And I'm very grateful," said Sam with a smile, "I really am."

Sam walked out of the office into the afternoon sunshine. A gleaming Triumph sports convertible was parked on the kerb outside. The roof was down and the interior was pristine. Sam pulled his sunglasses out of his pocket, as he admired the car and grinned. Then he opened the driver's door and climbed in.

The Speedway Couriers' office was a Portakabin living out its final days among bits of rusty machinery in a deserted tanner's yard. The main feature of the front office that afternoon was a skinny biker in scuffed leathers and a bandanna asleep in an old deck chair. His feet were extended in front of him; clad in a pair of muddy motocross boots, resting on a pile of bike magazines which had been stacked haphazardly on a low Formica coffee table. When the door slammed, it woke him up with a start.

Rosie, a butch twenty-year-old, dragged her mountain bike over the step and through the doorway. She wore a face mask, snazzy wraparound shades and was squeezed into top-to-toe protective Lycra. She hauled the bike across the room and leant it against the one flimsy wall of the cabin. She pulled down her face mask and slide her glasses onto the top of her head before walking purposefully over to where the biker slouched in his deck chair. A glossy calendar hung on a nail above his head, advertising motor oil. Partially anyway. Most of it was taken up with a photograph of a busty, heavily made-up blonde woman lying topless across the bonnet of an American hot rod. Rosie ripped the calendar off the wall in one smooth swipe.

"Eh? Leave it out, Rosie," mumbled the biker, stifling a yawn.

"It's about time," she said rummaging in the despatch bag that was slung over her shoulder, "that we had some art around here."

She pulled out a brand-new Chippendales' calendar and flipped fast through its glossy leaves to find the correct month. July displayed a picture of several Chippendales sipping elaborate and colourful cocktails. They were dressed only in their trademark bow ties; the rest was all shiny chestnut flesh and ivory teeth.

"No fucking way. We're not having that in here."

Rosie steadied herself, putting one hand on the biker's chest, then leaned across and hung the calendar carefully above his head.

"I dunno. They look like your sort of boys."

Charlie followed Rosie through the door. He was dressed in the cracked leathers of a courier. He wore a plastic Speedway Couriers' bib over the top of his jacket and a crackling, two-way radio hung across his right shoulder. Pulling off his helmet, he shook out his blond hair.

"All right, Rose. All right, Spider."

"Charlie."

He clumped past Rosie and the biker in his heavy boots and tapped a frosted-glass screen. The screen slid back to reveal a fat man in a sweaty nylon shirt. He was almost entirely bald but had smoothed a few strands of hair across his shiny pate. His little room was grey with smoke but that didn't stop him taking a drag on the cigarette end which he dwarfed between his fat fingers. He sat at a wooden desk on which he also rested part of his stomach. The tools of his trade, a radio mike, a telephone and a dog-eared orders book, shared the desk with his belly, as did the perks of his job: a can of warm Coca-Cola, an overflowing ashtray and an open copy of *Razzle*.

"Cheque?" said Charlie. The fat controller looked at him blankly. "You got my cheque?"

"Tomorrow," wheezed the controller from a thin, dry throat.

"It's my last fucking day, B."

"I need you tomorrow, 21."

"My name's Charlie and don't give me that 21 shit, B. I've got a photo shoot in two hours."

"Well fuck off then, 21. Just make sure you're here tomorrow."

Charlie turned to Rosie. She shrugged her shoulders. Behind her, the biker slowly reached above his head, trying to get a finger to the Chippendales calendar.

"Oi, fuck off," shouted Rosie, as she slapped him over the head with the hot rod girl's boobs.

"All right, B! One more day. But if my cheque's not here tomorrow, I'll come back and shove that radio up your arse."

The streets were packed as usual. A sunny day always brought the crowds out. Those who could afford it huddled around little tables outside the cafés while everyone else perched on walls and window-sills trying to catch a couple of tanning rays in their lunch break. Charlie took a sharp right off Old Compton Street into Wardour Street. A black cab slammed on its brakes with a metallic squeal. The driver barely had time to lean out his window and call him a wanker before Charlie had slipped up the side of the slow-moving line of traffic. He honked his horn every couple of yards to clear the pedestrians who had spilled off the narrow pavement and into his path. They shifted stiffly back onto the pavement all in their own rush to get to meetings in the bars and offices that made up the tight maze of Soho.

Charlie pulled up outside a converted shop front. There was a slight bend in the road which gave enough space for a few bike couriers to park up and wait for their next job. They sat on their bikes and talked, opening up their leathers to let the steam out. Some read tatty paperbacks or newspapers, others sipped coffee from styrofoam mugs. Charlie flicked out the kick stand of his bike with his foot and dismounted.

"Watch me bike for us, mate," he said to guy who lay along the top of his bike sunbathing.

"I'm only here a minute."

"I'm only going to be a minute."

"Yeah, all right."

"Cheers."

Charlie jogged across the road to a small blue door wedged between a pizza restaurant and the imposing mirrored windows of a film company. There were dozens of buttons on the intercom, each marked with a grand name. He rang one.

"Yes," it hummed.

"I'm here to see David. Pick up me portfolio."

"Okay, third floor."

The door buzzed and Charlie shoved it open. He found himself at the foot of a thin wooden staircase. The stairwell was gloomy and smelt of dust. He climbed quickly to the third floor, where he stopped in front of a pale wooden fire door. Charlie caught a glimpse of himself in its shatterproof glass. Speedway Couriers written all over him; hardly a byword in the fast-moving word of fashion. Reassessing his look, he unwound the radio from his neck and pulled off the plastic bib. He stuffed them both, along with his helmet and gloves, behind the fire door, which he wedged open with one of the rusted fire extinguishers which hung on the wall.

Charlie moved into the murky darkness of a short passageway. The door at the end of it had a David Alway's business card stuck to it with a blob of Blu-Tack. The card simply described him as 'Photographer'.

Charlie knocked. Almost immediately, the door opened a few inches to reveal the face of a pretty girl of about his age. She waved Charlie in.

David Alway's studio seemed huge in comparison to the muggy stairwell. Its walls were plain brick and what windows there were had been covered with heavy black felt. There were a couple of trestle tables standing against the far wall which slouched under the weight of contact sheets, light boxes, bottles of fluid and assorted cameras. A huge Fifties refrigerator shuddered in one corner. All attention was focused on a large white canvas which covered one entire wall. It flowed down from the ceiling and continued across the floor. On it stood an overstuffed paisley-patterned sofa. Laid across that was a stunning model in a revealing chiffon dress.

The model lay in a strange and uncomfortable position across its back. Around her was a tripod forest of freestanding lights and cameras of all sizes. Various assistants and accessories hung around; some watched avidly, other sat on flight cases and contemplated their navels. David Alway was a tall man in his forties dressed with causal glamour in a loose-fitting white cotton shirt and chinos. He stood behind the camera flanked by an assistant with a light meter.

"Lovely. Just look left a bit. Chin up. Alison, mess her hair up a bit."

The girl who opened the door to Charlie dashed over to the model and went to work with a comb. One of the men sitting on a flight case looked up from the sheaf of notes he was reading and asked Charlie his name.

"Charlie Rowntree. I'm here to pick up my portfolio." The man nodded with recognition.

"Wait here."

The man walked over to David Alway and whispered in his ear. Alway whispered back from the side of his mouth.

"You're not getting it, Atlanta," he continued. "Think about the first time you fell in love."

The assistant returned. "Your portfolio's over there." He pointed to one of the trestle tables and then continued with his notes.

"Never fallen in love? What about your first roll in the hay then, eh?"

The model remained impassive.

Charlie couldn't quite believe what he'd heard. He had expected at least a word of encouragement, some acknow-ledgement that what was in the portfolio had some potential. As he picked up his portfolio off the table he let his eyes burn into David Alway's back. Ten years of his work flushed down the drain and the bastard hadn't even had the balls to tell he wasn't interested himself. Charlie wanted to smack him in the mouth.

"Whoever this lover boy was he can't have been that good. Come on!"

Charlie was still fuming as he headed for the door. As he walked behind the photographer, Alway turned away from his camera to catch Charlie's eye.

"Did you print those yourself?" he asked.

"Yeah."

The photographer turned back to the model.

"Think about the money then, Atalanta. I know you love money." The photographer paused as if in thought. "Start Monday morning, seven dead. Don't be late."

"What?" said Charlie stunned. "You don't mean . . .?"

"Yes, now fuck off, see you Monday."

Charlie felt drunk as he walked to the door. Every good thing that had ever happened to him had been distilled into one triumphant moment. Grinning from ear to ear, he took a final look at the studio, his new place of work. He saw the model was looking at him. He gave her a flirty wink. She smiled.

"That's it!" cried the photographer.

Charlie let himself out.

3

"Best thing about this place," started Bobby as she licked the tip of her finger and flicked through a pile of twenties for the second time. She dropped the small stack of notes into a metal drawer in front of her and pushed it shut. On the other side of the window a customer picked up his money. "Thank you, have a nice weekend." The customer walked away without a word. "Don't get run over by a bus," said Bobby under her breath.

"What is it?" said Rachel.

"What is what?"

"The best thing about working here. Because I can't think of anything."

"Friday night," said Bobby.

"Oh," said Rachel. "So it's not the twenty-one days' paid holiday a year, on-site training and subsidised mortgage plan."

"Fuck off," said Bobby. "This best thing about working here is knowing at this time on a Friday night, I'm no more than thirty minutes away from a big spliff and a weekend of wine, *men* and song."

Rachel laughed.

"Everything all right?" Mr Finch appeared, uncomfortably close, behind them.

"Yes, Mr Finch," they chorused.

"Good, let's finish up here. I'm sure you've both got good-looking boyfriends waiting for you at home."

Bobby and Rachel grimaced at each other.

The building society manager was a real letch, all straying hands and furtive looks down the front of the blouse. The rumour was that he was happily married, a wife and kids apparently, though nobody had ever seen them. One of the security guards claimed that he had seen him in town once with some right old tug boat. Still, the same guard had also claimed to be the 1978 World Judo Champion. Whatever Mr

Finch's domestic arrangements were, they was no excuse to get so smarmy over the female employees.

Sure enough at six o'clock he was waiting to unlock the front door when Bobby and Rachel were ready to leave. Mr Finch held the door open for them, jiggling the keys with his free hand.

"See you Monday, girls."

"See you Monday, Mr Finch."

He patted Bobby on the bum as she walked past.

"Don't do anything I wouldn't do."

Bobby smiled sarcastically.

Out in the street the sun was shining and the late afternoon smog had turned the high road a hazy yellow. Mr Finch closed the heavy glass doors behind them, shutting out another week of fixed-rate endowments and gold saver plans.

"That *fucking* letch. He does that every week."

"Just ignore him," said Rachel as she linked arms with Bobby. "Bet his dick's as small as his brain" She laughed. "Quick drink?"

"I'd better not," said Bobby. "Boy Wonder's coming to pick me up."

Further down the road Bobby spotted Sherry coming out of a chemist. She looked far from happy. Her face was blank, she was in a daze. As she walked across pavement she dragged her feet behind her as if she was exhausted. She sat down heavily on a bus shelter red plastic bench. Bobby took a step forward to get a better view. Sherry had dropped her head in her hands. Sherry's shoulders began to heave as she sobbed.

"You know her?" asked Rachel.

"Yeah, look . . . see you tomorrow night, yeah?"

"Sure, later." Rachel turned and head off down the street.

Bobby walked swiftly up the road, dodging shoppers until she reached Sherry.

"Sherry?" Sherry looked up. There were two silver tear lines down her face.

"Oh, Bobby."

"What's up?" said Bobby, putting her arm around Sherry.

"I'm late."

34

"You're what?"

"Late. As in my mum's going to kill me. As in Rix is going to leave me. As in stuck in some poky fucking council flat rotting away for the rest of my fucking life late!"

"You're pregnant?"

Sherry nodded. She opened her handbag. Inside there was a home pregnancy tester.

"I was meant to do this test. But I just can't, Bobby. I'm too scared."

Sam pulled up in his Triumph, fresh from the dole office. He honked the horn.

"Come on. We're going to be late." He leant across to open the passenger door and pushed it wide open. Sherry dabbed at her eyes with a paper hanky. "All right, Sherry?"

Sherry nodded and forced a smile.

"Why don't you come with us?"

"I can't. I'm going home."

"Okay. We'll sort it out, all right."

Sherry grabbed Bobby's arm as she moved to go. "Don't say nothing!"

"Course I won't."

Bobby jumped into the front and gave Sam a fat kiss on the cheek.

"Girly chat?" he said.

"Something like that."

The gravel of the driveway gave a deep growl as Sam fish-tailed the Triumph off the road and brought it to a halt in front of his garage. Sam's house was a large Victorian number in Greenwich's leafy suburbs. Half-million-pound houses for stockbrokers and accountants. It was his mum's really but she was never there, choosing instead to spend nearly all her time at her boyfriend's place in Henley-on-Thames. It suited Sam right down to the ground. Twenty-one-years-old, driving a sports classic into the driveway of his four-bedroom detached house. A swimming pool and cable TV and dear old mummy turning up once a fortnight to fill the fridge. Life was sweet, this place was theirs all summer. Bobby gave a cheer and kissed

Sam on the cheek as she climbed out of the car and ran towards the house.

"You coming?" called Bobby over her shoulder.

"Just a sec," said Sam. Right ahead of him were the closed doors of his garage. Behind them he could hear the odd notes and muttered arrangements of the band tuning up. Sam leant across and opened the polished-wood door of the Triumph's glove compartment. He pulled out a crumpled packet of Silk Cut. Inside were two ready-rolled joints; he took one out and stuck it in his mouth, lighting it with a plastic Bic lighter. Leaning back against the smooth leather of his seat, he waited for the show.

Sam's garage had been converted into a makeshift studio. Garden tools, pool inflatables and sacks of lawn fertiliser had been pushed back against its walls to make room for a huge mixing desk and a set of Technics turntables which Rix had set up on top of the black and silver flight cases they came in. The centrepiece of the set-up was an electronic keyboard on stiff steel legs. The floor was covered with thick rubber wires which spewed out from the back of Rix's console. Some of them snaked over to lethal-looking clumps of plugs which hung off ancient, dusty sockets. Others made their way to the microphone and practice amps which were arranged on the concrete floor. A pale wood bass guitar was propped against one wall. Various stools and garden chairs were dotted around for spectators. On every available surface there stood ashtrays full of crushed joint stubs and half-drunk cups of coffee.

"Now this is from the top," said Rix, fixing Bean with a serious gaze over the top of his knobs and switches. "Keep it tight."

Bean nodded and tapped his fingers eagerly along the keys of his trumpet. He sucked on his lips as if he had something caught in his teeth; then put the mouthpiece to his lips. Taking a huge breath, he played a stunning scale which rose and rose until it hit a high C that filled the room; a cool, calm note that could cut glass.

"Yeah!" shouted Rix. Swinging his arms wildly as if calling

the music on, he flicked a switch which dropped a solid electronic beat behind Bean's trumpeting. "Here we go."

Rix picked up his headphones. No longer a permanent feature of his Walkman, they had found a new home plugged into the top of his decks. Pressing one earpiece to his head with the flat of his hand, he set a record in motion. It was a loop of chattering urban sounds which provided an essential texture to his rough beats.

Bean started up again. This time his playing was slower and less dramatic. His melody was chatty, almost like speech.

Rix dropped the headphones around his neck and, bending low over the mixing desk, he began to work on the levels, his eyes fixed with a ferocious intensity on the dancing dials in front of him.

Bobby pulled open the door, letting a shock of sunlight into the gloom. The music stopped dead.

"At last," said Rix looking up.

"Hello, boys."

Bean played a little fanfare on his trumpet.

"All right, Bobby," he said with a smile.

Bobby took a seat on a stool next to his. She plucked the bass guitar from against the wall and slung its leather strap around her neck. Checking it was plugged in, she plucked her first tentative notes.

"Too mechanical . . . Get into a groove," said Rix.

"Give her a second to warm up," said Bean.

"S'all right, Bean." Bobby began to slap out a rhythm with her outstretched thumb; the kind of rhythm that would make your grandmother want to dance. She upped the tempo. "How's that?"

Rix gave her a double thumbs-up and then joined in on the keyboard. Bean's trumpet spoke over the top, a unique and mellow improvisation.

"What's this?" Sam strode in with a joint hanging from his lips. The trio, absorbed in music, didn't hear him. He walked over to a clump of plugs and pulled it out of the wall. Everything went dead. The three players looked up from their instruments in surprise. "What the fuck is this?"

he demanded. He walked right up to Bean and glared at him.

"What the fuck is what?" said Bean.

"This! We wanna sell records, not fucking give them away."

"Who asked you?"

"Who asked me?" said Sam as he flushed with indignant rage. "I'm your fucking manager! You know, the geezer who made all this happen, who bought all this equipment, who gave you all those CDs you listen to." He turned and looked at Rix. "Who sorted you out with all those records to sample." Rix hung his head in embarrassment. "Just keep doing what you were doing, okay."

"We were improvising" said Bean. "Doing what we do best, being creative."

"Well stop it," Sam shouted. He shoved the plug back into its socket for emphasis.

The door of the garage opened again. It was Sherry, still puffy around the eyes. She had changed into her swimming costume and now had Lucy in tow.

"Look what the cat dragged in."

"Sorry I'm late," said Lucy. "Charlie back yet?" There was a pause. Lucy grimaced, sensing the atmosphere. "Bad time?"

"Nah," said Sam. "Sorting out a few artistic differences." He passed his joint to Bean in reconciliation. Bean waved the joint away.

"Not for me, Charlie said he's coming to take photos . . ."

"How the fuck do you think Jimi-fucking-Hendrix wrote *Electric Ladyland*, eh? It wasn't by drinking fucking lemonade, mate. Now, smoke it!" Bean smirked.

"You're the manager." He took the joint.

"Okay," said Rix. "Let's try again. He put his headphones on and restarted the beat.

Sherry went over to the mixing desk. Slipping behind it she put her arms around Rix and nibbled his neck.

"Sherry!" said Rix. She hugged him harder and carried on nibbling. "Sherry!" Rix was angry. He shrugged her off and pulled off his earphones. "I'm trying to work."

"Sorry to disturb you," said Sherry, hurt. "I was just being affectionate. She slid out from behind the mixing desk and sat herself down in a garden chair. She folded her arms and sucked her teeth at Rix.

From outside came the throaty sound of a motorcycle engine. The familiar footsteps of Charlie's heavy biker boots clumped down the concrete path that ran along the side of the garage. The footsteps stopped outside the closed garage door. The door swung slowly open to reveal Charlie on the threshold, gunfighter style, silhouetted in the sunlight. Rix killed the music. Charlie, still decked out in leathers and courier bib, took two deliberate steps into the garage.

"For years there's been peace." He pointed at Bean, then let his finger trace slowly around the room. "I've put money in all your pockets. But now someone's got greedy."

"*Long Good Friday*," said Bean.

Charlie slapped five with him. "Oh," he said, feigning forgetfulness. "I remember there was some talk of me doing some photos for you this afternoon."

"Yeah," said Bean eagerly.

"Well, I'd like to, but I'm just not sure you can afford me." Charlie paused, "Not now I'm a professional."

"You got it," shouted Lucy. She leapt up and threw her arms around his neck.

"Yeah, beautiful girls, top threads, exotic locations. No money, but who gives a fuck?" He looked around at the others, who were still on edge after their argument. "Well, don't rush me!" he said.

Bean, Rix, Sherry and Bobby crowded round Charlie, patting him on the back and congratulating him.

"Nice one."

"Knew you could do it, mate," said Bean. He turned to Sam. "See, Sam. Creative."

Sam remained aloof, his managerial cool blown by Charlie's good fortune. Charlie stopped and looked at Sam.

"I didn't mean it about the money, mate," he said with a cheeky smile.

Sam smiled back. "You cunt." He gave Charlie a hug.

"Come Monday things are going to be very different

for your uncle Charlie." He grabbed Lucy and gave her a big kiss. "Speaking of creative, I've got a great idea for you lot."

Charlie took Bean, Rix and Bobby down to the docks. He led the way on his bike, giving arm signals to Sam in his Triumph, who struggled to keep up with the twists and turns of Charlie's convoluted courier's route. There was no trouble getting into the docks themselves. They were virtually disused now and had yet to be converted into high-rent apartments for the yuppies in Docklands. Every now and then some huge freighter would squeeze through the Thames barrier and off-load a dozen or so salt-bitten containers of God knows what onto waiting lorries. Primo-grade Mexican loco weed, Charlie always claimed, but it was more likely car parts or Swedish furniture. Business was nothing like what it was. Nowadays the docks were just a dangerous place for kids to play or a free canvas for the local graffiti artists to practise their tags.

Charlie spent ages setting the three of them up against the rusty flank of a disused crane. The scene was perfect urban decay; all twisted metal and hanging chains. Sam busied himself with suggestions and unwanted advice about the band's 'look'.

When Charlie had finally finished setting his camera he said, "Right. Just the band members please."

Sam looked up. "Er, anyone want a bang on this?" He held out a smouldering joint to Bean, who again waved him off.

"Fuck off, Sam," said Charlie from behind the camera. "I know what I want here and it ain't the paranoid look. I want south London attitude."

"How the fuck do you think John Lennon wrote *Imagine*, eh?" said Sam. "I say they all have a big toke. Paranoia. That's where it's at."

"Sam, make yourself useful. Go climb a tree or something?"

Sam strode off, muttering to himself.

Charlie looked through the viewfinder of his camera. Rix, Bean and Bobby came into focus, standing out sharply against the peeling paint and corroded metal of the crane's huge leg.

Charlie winced at the sight. They had failed to grasp his instructions and stood in a tight huddle with their arms folded. They looked like a set of angry school teachers.

"No, no, no," said Charlie. "That ain't attitude, that's staring." Charlie stepped out from behind his camera and walked over to his reluctant subjects. He pulled them roughly into place. Returning to his position behind the camera, he checked the viewfinder. Now they looked like a bunch of ragdolls. They stood unnaturally in the exact positions Charlie had put them in. He sighed.

"You don't do this often, do ya?"

"Eh?" they said.

Charlie looked around him, trying to seek some inspiration. He turned around and looked across the river. There was Canary Wharf, London's very own Empire State towering above them like a giant silver monolith. "Perfect," he said under his breath. He took position behind the camera again.

"Listen to me. See that office building, Canary Wharf?"

"Yeah," came the reply.

"Focus on the glass pyramid at the top." Their eyes climbed the huge silver monolith. "At the centre of that pyramid is the answer to the big one. The scary one. Life. With a capital 'L'."

Bean, Bobby and Rix begin to relax. As they focused on the tower their eyes clouded with a thoughtful distance; distance or their naive hope and burning ambition. Charlie saw his plan was working.

"Now you're in the lift. Going up . . . up . . . up . . . You're looking out and all of London is laid at your feet. You're moving faster and faster. Getting closer and closer to the top. In front of you is the emergency stop button. The question I want you to ask yourself is this. Do you want to ride all the way to the top . . . or would you rather live out your life in total ignorance?"

"The top," said Bobby.

"All the way," said Rix.

"Fuck yeah!" said Bean.

And the shutter clicked.

41

4

Bean's dad, Brian, sat on the dirty sofa of their council flat. The place was decorated like a granny's flat, with floral-pattern wallpaper and china ornaments on the window-sills. That was Brian's wife. He hadn't touched anything since she passed away. The surfaces were covered in a thin layer of dust. The whole house smelt of fags and sweat. Brian's tatty check shirt was open to the waist to reveal a swollen beer belly held in by a string vest. Two of his cronies from the site sat with him. All of them had fags on the go and were drinking beer from a selection of cans sat on the coffee table in front of them. Brian also nipped from a quarter-bottle of cheap Scotch he held loosely in one hand. In the corner a football match blared from the television set.

"This boy really got some talent," said Brian's mate, sucking hard on his fag.

"Bollocks," said Brian with unusual spite. "He's a fucking shit stabber." Brian stood up and pointed at the television with his bottle. "Look at him. Look at the way he's running. The poor bastard's jacksie's killing him!" Brian sat down as his mates cracked up.

"Bet you Schmeichel's been up there, the dirty fucker," said Brian's mate.

The muffled sound of Bean's trumpet came through the ceiling. He was playing scales. Brian's face turned a terrible puce.

"For fuck's sake. The cunt knows I hate that shit." He pulled off his slipper and stood up to hammer on the ceiling with its flat rubber heel. "Oi, Bean. Shut it. Shut the fuck up now!" The music stopped. "Thank Christ for that." Then the music continued. This time it was louder and faster. Bean's trademark scale rising to a deafening high C.

"Jesus," said Brian's mate.

"That fucking wanker!" seethed Brian. He stormed out of the room.

43

Bean sat on the end of his neatly made bed. His room, unlike the rest of the flat, was clean and tidy. The walls were covered with black and white pictures of jazz greats cut out of magazines. Most of them were smiling, decked out in sharp suits and proudly holding their instruments on their laps. Bean crouched by the side of his bed and pointed his trumpet like a weapon directly through the floor at Brian's head below. He blared another scale.

Satisfied, Bean stopped playing and wiped his lips with the back of his hand. He went to put his trumpet carefully back in its case. He didn't noticed Brian's footsteps on the stairs outside his room, but he couldn't fail to spot his face, flushed red with drunken fury, as he broke in through the door.

"What did I fucking tell you?" he shouted.

Bean stared into Brian's bloodshot eyes.

"Dunno."

"What did I tell you about playing that shit in my house?" he bellowed.

"Mum used to like it" said Bean quietly.

"You shut it about that bitch."

"You gonna put me in intensive care too, are you?" spat Bean.

"You fucking little queer!"

"She said you couldn't get it up anyway."

Brian's growled. His fist came out of nowhere, a blur of white knuckles. It contacted Bean's face and sent him spinning sideways back across his bed. Bean floundered for a second. Then he pulled his trumpet across the counterpane towards him. He curled up over his instrument as the blows rained down.

5

Charlie was in his darkroom. It was really a larder that his Dad had helped him to convert. He'd tacked felt around the edges of the door and put in a couple of red light bulbs. All it took after that was a decorator's table and a couple of his mum's washing lines. Trays of developing solution sat on the table. Rows of developed pictures hung from the remaining free space.

Charlie leant over the first of pictures from that afternoon's shoot. He moved it gently around in the flat tray of finishing solution with a pair of plastic tongs. Outside he heard the doorbell ring.

"Can you get that, Mum?" he shouted. "I'm right in the middle of it." The picture began to appear through the liquid. Bean, Rix and Bobby. Their eyes were distant but full of some unseen life force. They looked dynamic and fresh against the background of decay. The light reflected from the river had given them an almost translucent quality.

The door opened a crack, letting a blade of light cut through the gloom.

"Mum," pleaded Charlie. "The prints."

"Sorry, love. Bean's here. His dad's only gone and thrown him out for good."

Charlie pushed past his mother into the hall still holding the photograph with the plastic tweezers. Bean stood in the hall with his head bowed. He was carrying a small overnight bag and his trumpet case. As he looked up Charlie saw one of his eyes was half closed and purple with swelling. His lip was fat and there was a thin dark cut across its smooth pink flesh.

"That fucking wanker!" shouted Charlie.

"It's all right, Bean, love. You can stay here as long as you like," said Charlie's mum, touching Bean on the arm.

"Thanks, Mrs Jackson," said Bean quietly.

"I'll put the kettle on, then I'll make up the spare room." She hurried away down the corridor.

"I'm going to fucking sort that fat bastard out. So help me, I'm going to fucking kill him," said Charlie.

"Is that our photos?" said Bean.

"Yeah," said Charlie, taken aback. He lifted up the tweezers and handed the photograph to Bean. "Three faces full of ignorance, happy at the endless possibilities of life," he said.

Bean took the photograph and looked at it. His face lit up. "Look at us, Charlie. We look kind of . . . famous."

Charlie dropped a contact sheet on the wooden picnic table set up at the end of Sam's garden. Rix grabbed it eagerly.

"Oi!" said Sam as he snatched it out of Rix's hands. "I'm the manager. How about a bit of professional respect?"

"Plenty to go round, boys," said Charlie. He unzipped the big artist's portfolio bag he had brought with him and slid twenty or so developed photographs onto the table.

"These are brilliant!" said Bobby.

"Looks even better from over here. Lucky you got me as manager, Bob," said Sam.

Charlie straightened and put his hand on Sam's shoulder.

"Yeah, Sam. Nice choice of shutter speed and light fraction. I really like the way you've worked with the subject."

Sam flushed. "Yeah well. Like I say. Nice one."

"Nice one! Nice is like rice – bland. Give me the sauce! Give me wicked, Charlie. Well done, Charlie!"

"Well done, Charlie," said Bobby putting her arm round his shoulders. She gave him a peck on the cheek.

"*Thank you! At last.*"

"These are brilliant, mate," said Rix with a sloppy grin.

"I gotta show this one to Sherry and Lucy," said Bobby. She picked up a picture and ran across the lawn to where the girls were sunbathing.

Sam examined the pictures, feigning an expert's eye.

"Yeah, Uncle Henry is going to love this . . ."

A couple of drops of water fell on the photograph in front of him. "Eh?" Then another full squirt hit him in the eye. "What the fuck?" Sam caught sight of Rix's six-year-old sister, Ani. Her huge hair stuck out from behind the shrub.

"Ani . . ." he shouted. She jumped out with a huge gap-toothed grin. She was dressed in a one-piece bathing costume and had an evil-looking water pistol in one hand. "Rix, sort your sister out! I thought you were taking her home."

"It's you she's in love with, mate. You take her home."

Sam jumped up and chased the squealing Ani across the lawn. He finally caught her and, despite her screams for mercy, dropped her in the pool, splashing water over Lucy, Sherry and Bobby, who were busy examining the photograph.

"Oi!" they screamed, wiping their suntan-oil-smeared bodies. "Sam!"

Ani popped up at the side of the pool red-eyed and coughing, but none the less all smiles.

"Listen," said Sam. "If you get dressed real quick, I'll take you home in my car."

"Roof down?"

"Roof down."

Ani scrabbled out of the pool and ran towards the house.

The three girls sat at the end of the pool with their feet dangling in the cool water.

"So, what's your mum going to say?" asked Lucy. She exhaled a lung full of smoke and passed the joint along to Sherry.

"Quite a lot I should think," said Bobby. "What are you going to do?"

Sherry sighed.

"Dunno. Eat till I'm grossly overweight. Throw up every morning. Grow tits bigger than Dolly Parton . . ."

"Complain of backache every five minutes because you've got a weight like a bag of cement strapped round your middle . . ." continued Lucy.

"Scream abuse at the midwife and beg for every drug under the sun," said Bobby with a grin.

Sherry handed the joint on.

"Try to squeeze a ten-pound wrinkled pink thing out of a hole that's had nothing larger than a gherkin pass through it?"

"God!" said Bobby. "I thought Rix was a bit bigger than that."

The girls cracked up.

Ani came running out of the house now fully dressed.

"What's so funny?" she said.

"Nothing," said Sherry, "just talking about gherkins."

"I don't like gherkins, they're horrible" said Ani.

The girls cracked up again.

"Well, I wish someone had told me that a lot sooner, darling," said Sherry. "Come on, let's find Sam." Sherry took hold of Ani's hand.

"You know there are options, Sherry," said Bobby.

"Bobby!" scolded Lucy.

Sherry looked down at Ani with a strange melancholy. After a second she looked back at her friends and in a quiet voice said, "I don't think so."

"Oi! If you want to smoke that shit in my car you can fucking walk." The cab driver flapped the newspaper he was reading at Rix's smoke cloud with both hands.

"All right, mate. Keep your wig on," said Rix. He dropped the joint on the ground and stubbed it out under his trainer. The driver sat in the first of the two battered Ford Mondeos, which passed for minicabs, parked at the end of Sam's drive.

"Thanks a lot, Rix," said Sam, coming out of the house with Charlie. Sam was wearing a purple silk suit and tie, Charlie was less formal in a Hawaiian shirt and jeans. "I'm sure my mum'd love to see your roaches littering up her drive the next time she turns up."

"If she turns up. She's never here. That's why we all love her."

"Show a bit of respect, eh?"

Rix picked up the joint stub and tossed it into some bushes.

Charlie patted Rix on the back. He opened the cab's back door and climbed in.

"So if we're off to meet the music industry's favourite turd burglar, don't you think you should sort out a name for the band?"

"What do you think about *Rising Tide*?" said Rix, following him into the cab.

48

"Too pretentious," said Charlie.

"I'm not asking you. I'm asking my manager. What do you think, Sam?" Sam shrugged.

"Dunno. When the right one hits, we'll know it . . . like naming a baby. Like if Sherry was pregnant."

"Leave it out."

Sam climbed into the front seat of the first cab and addressed the cab driver: "You know where we're going? *Cutty Sark*, right?"

"Yeah."

Charlie was laughing and poking Rix in the ribs.

"Papa Rix." Rix wriggled in the seat next to him. "If Sherry was pregnant, he'd shit himself," said Charlie.

"Fucking right I would! Fucking kids, fuck that!"

Sam turned around to face them. "Settle down now, children. So, you wouldn't have one then? What's the matter with you? Don't you love her?"

"Course I fucking wouldn't . . . what are you on about?"

"Just checking."

Bean, Lucy and Sherry appeared at the cab window. Bean and Lucy were chattering away. But Sherry stayed silent, giving Rix a look through the open car door. Up at the house, Bobby finally emerged from the doorway. She smiled and blew Sam a kiss.

Behind him, Rix was still laughing.

"Yeah, yeah! Now I get it. You and Bobby's thinking about it!"

"Rix," said Sam. "You can fuck right off."

The *Cutty Sark* towered above them, its huge masts disappearing into the night sky. It was a full-size clipper ship, one of eight 'sisters' built for the tea trade with China; an enormous construction of rope, wood and iron that had been round the world and back only to find itself rigging, mast, keel and all dry-docked in sea of cobbles for the benefit of generations of American tourists. Looking at it still took your breath away; the romance of a hundred childhood pirate movies.

Tonight the ship was heaving with people. Sam's godfather

and uncle, Henry Knight, may have been the campest old queen in London but he also ran one of its most successful music management companies; and he knew how to throw a party. Coloured lights had been strung along the ship's rigging and a makeshift stage, complete with spark machines and lasers, had been erected at the stern. There were bars on the port and starboard sides flanked by Dionysian ice statues. A huge banner was hung down one side of the hull which read *South East Management* in big bold lettering. On board a fashionable crowd thronged across the decks, sipping champagne and swigging from beer bottles.

Sam stood proudly in front of the ship waiting for the others to settle with the cab drivers. He smiled broadly. This was his party.

"Now stay cool and stay with me, right?" he said. "I've only got one ticket."

"You what?" said Charlie.

"Don't sweat it." Sam put his arm round Charlie's shoulders. "I always sort me mates out."

"Speaking of getting sorted." Rix pulled a flat wrap of silver foil out of his pocket. He unfolded it to reveal tabs of flecked white ecstasy.

"Now you're talking," said Charlie. He grabbed two and popped one in Lucy's mouth and one in his own.

"Later, yeah." Sam walked towards a long queue which had formed in front of the ship's gangplank.

"Sherry?" Rix offered her one.

"Fuck off . . . Come on, Bobby." She linked her arm through Bobby's and pulled her after Sam.

"Don't fucking diss me, then walk away!"

"I told you to stop taking that shit," she said over her shoulder. "Now grow up."

Rix looked at Bean, who shrugged and went after the girls.

"Bollocks," said Rix.

Two tough-looking bouncers in dinner suits stood at the head of the queue along with another man in a black polo neck and a long black coat. He held a clipboard and was speaking into a walkie-talkie. Sam walked straight up to him and presented his ticket. The man turned the ticket over in his hands, then looked up at Sam.

"In you go then." Sam moved forward, waving his friends with him. "Hey," said the man with the walkie-talkie. "What's this?"

"They're my guests," said Sam.

"I don't think so."

"I'm Sam Jackson . . . Henry Knight's nephew, and these are my guests."

"And that," said the man, pointing with his walkie-talkie, ". . . is the guest queue, all right?"

"'Aving a liccle bit a trouble?" said a voice behind Sam. He turned to see Elroy, who had forced his way to the front of the queue. Elroy hardly looked like the podgy teenager Sam remembered. He was smartly dressed in true yardie style, a long black leather coat with a heavy gold chain hanging round his neck and a row of gold sovereign rings spread across the fingers of one of his hands; he held a mobile phone in the other.

"Fuck mine. It's a class reunion," he said, looking around Sam's assembled group.

"Elroy. What the fuck do you want."

"Nuttin' you can help me with." Elroy turned to Bean. "Now now, Mistah Bean! How's me bredren from the concrete jungle?"

"All right Elroy," said Bean with a smile.

"I don't believe this," said Sam.

Elroy tinged his voice with a heavy Jamaican accent.

"Sam Jackson. The golden bwoy. Things have changed. You see, me is making a *dishonest* living now and I is going up in the world, you get me?" He touched fists with one of the bouncers and walked onto the boat. He stopped on the gangplank. "Bean, you wan' anything, you call me, aye?"

Bean nodded. Elroy disappeared into the party.

"Shit, did you see that?" said Bean.

"This is well out of fucking order." Sam sighed and put his hands in his pockets.

Rix was examining Charlie's photo of the band.

"This is great, Charlie, I mean really top. But we gotta get a better name."

"Yeah, you're right. Sam, what about *Meantime*?"

"Name? Fuck the name," said Sam, still furious at being upstaged by Elroy.

"Chill out, Sam," said Bobby. "We'll just wait a little bit."

"Ain't that your uncle?" said Rix, pointing up at the ship's deck.

Sam looked up to see Uncle Henry leaning on the ship's railing. He wore a flamboyantly cut green suit with a huge carnation in his buttonhole. Surrounded by a group of well-dressed young men, he laughed and joked, gesticulating with a glass of champagne.

"Oi, Henry," shouted Sam.

Henry looked down with a grand sneer. "Sam! What are you doing down there?"

"Look, I brought the posse." Sam gestured over his shoulder at the others.

"Well, get your pretty little asses up here."

The bouncer stepped back and they shuffled single file across the gangplank.

The party was raging. It was a wild crowd. Women in cocktail dresses, swimsuits and miniskirts and men dressed even more outrageously in everything from black tie to leather chaps. A band sporting matching blue mohican haircuts thrashed out a tune on stage.

"Fuck mine," said Bean, looking around. "This is a little fruity."

"Loosen up, Bean," said Lucy. She grabbed him by his boyish cheeks. "Have a good time."

"Leave it out, Luce," said Charlie. "You keep doing that and he'll stick that way."

"Come on, let's go meet Henry," said Sam. "You'd better give me those pictures."

Rix nervously checked through their folder for the demo tape and Charlie's photo of the band, then handed them over.

They had to fight their way through the crowd to the upper deck, where Henry held court.

"Sam, my gorgeous nephew!" crooned Henry as they appeared from below. "Oh! And the whole gang. Dear Bobby. And Charlie, Lucy, Rix. How delightful." Bean steeped out from behind the others.

"Bean. Good gracious what happened to your eye?"

"What the fuck is Elroy doing here?" said Sam angrily. "We had to queue and he just walked in."

"Who's Elroy?"

"That cunt there!" Sam pointed down at Elroy, who stood at the bar.

"Well, my darling, he provides a service which makes my guests very happy. And that makes me happy. Now, where's your mum?"

"She might come later."

"I've heard that before."

"Make yourselves at home, everybody, and try not to behave yourselves," Henry said magnanimously. "I'm afraid I shall have to borrow my dear godson as I've got some people he simply has to meet." Henry turned to Sam. "Come with me."

Charlie rolled his shoulders as the first flickers of his ecstasy tab came alive.

"Hello, here's something. A bit of a boogie I think." He took Lucy's hand and pulled her towards the dance floor.

"We're going for a dance!" she announced.

Sherry looked at the grim-faced Rix. "I think I'll join you" she said. "You coming, Bob?"

"Sure."

"Sherry!" said Rix to her back as she walked off. He watched her disappear down to the main deck. "I don't get that girl sometimes." Bean smiled weakly. "I tell you, I'm seriously thinking about binning her."

"What?" said Bean.

"Look at me, Bean. Right on the brink of something big and she's treating me like a fucking kid."

"Come on, Rix, Sherry's brilliant."

"I've been going out with the same bird for eight years, Bean. It's time to move on."

"But don't you love her?"

"I don't know any more, mate, I really don't." Rix looked over the railing at the dance floor below. Sherry was nowhere to be seen. "Look. I'm sorry for dumping this on you, mate. I'm gonna go and sort this out."

Bean was left on his own. He made his way down to one of the bars and stood vacantly beside it for a while. A barman popped up next to him. He was lifting a lid under the bar to pull out a chilled bottle of champagne from a hidden ice chest.

"Next time you want to try ducking, mate," he said, spotting Bean's black eye.

"Yeah, cheers."

The barman disappeared off to the other end of the bar, filling glasses as he went.

"Champagne, Mr McCormack?" Bean asked himself. He leant over the bar and into the ice chest. "Don't mind if I do." He pulled out a bottle.

Henry drained his glass.

"Wake up, Sam. You and your mum won't have anything left unless you do something!"

"We'll sort it out . . ."

"Sort it out? Listen to you, Sam. I love you dearly but you two couldn't sort out a trip to Sainsbury's. You're going to have to do better than that."

"I am doing something better than that," said Sam. "I'm doing what Dad did, what you do. That's why I sent you the tape. I've got this to go with it too." Sam opened the folder and pulled at the photograph. Henry took the picture and glanced at it. He closed his eyes and sighed with frustration.

"I told you, Sam, you need a vocalist." He handed the photograph back. "Look, just enjoy the party. We'll talk about this later."

A man tapped Henry on the shoulder. He had short-cropped hair and wore a band T-shirt tucked into a pair of jeans.

" 'Ello, 'ello."

"Anthony. Dear boy!" said Henry.

"How's tricks?"

"Gorgeous as ever. Still got your sixth sense for talent?"

"Keep stealing before the rest can even smell it! You know me."

"Have you met my nephew? Sam, this is 'Buzz' Harris."
Sam shook his hand.

"Rough line records, A&R," said Buzz.

"A&R, eh? Looking for new bands."

"Always looking."

"Well, check this lot out. They're gonna be huge and you're the first to see them." Sam handed Buzz the photograph. "This lot does it all. Electric, acoustic, twelve-string, banjo . . . even a fucking trumpet."

"Oh yeah, what are they called?" asked Buzz.

Sam felt a knot of panic in his throat.

"Greenwich. Greenwich Mean Time. Er . . . G.M.T."

"Cool," said Ant, nodding his head. "Which one's the vocalist?"

Sam felt sick, his mind racing. Henry watched Sam with growing amusement.

"Yes, Sam, which one is the vocalist? I forget."

"The vocalist . . . Right. Well, we're laying down instrumental tracks right now. Jazz jungle. Real cutting-edge shit. But from next week we lay down the vocals . . . We got this great girl. Jade. Beautiful voice . . . great body."

Henry raised an eyebrow.

"I've got a tape . . ." started Sam, reaching into the folder.

"I'll take that," said Henry, as he plucked the tape out of Sam's hands. "I wouldn't want my nephew bothering you with business, Buzz. This is a party after all."

"I'll run a tape over," said Sam, crestfallen.

"Wicked. I'll look forward to it."

"Now, Buzz," said Henry, taking him by the arm, "I believe you wanted me to introduce you to a young man in the recreational retail business."

Buzz and Henry moved off into the party.

"Chip off the old block, eh, Henry," said Buzz as they moved away.

Henry laughed and shook his head. "Fucking kids."

Sherry and Bobby sat on the edge of the stage sipping their champagne and watching the dancers.

"Why'd you have to go and tell Sam, Bob?"

"I never told him!" said Bobby, outraged.

"What about that stuff they were talking about in the car? About naming kids and that." Bobby smiled.

"The kid they were naming was our beloved band, Sherry."

"Eh?"

"They were thinking of a name for the band."

"Oh," said Sherry.

"You know you've got to sort this out, Sherry, or you'll go nuts."

Sherry nodded.

"You've got to tell Rix."

"Yeah, I know."

"Just look at him."

On the other side of the dance floor, Rix was brooding. All around him the crowd laughed and chattered. He took occasional short swigs from a beer bottle. "He really loves you, you know."

"He's just pissed off cause he can't take his 'E'."

"Oh, come on, Sherry."

"I know. I'm sorry." Sherry knocked back her drink. "It's just, I wanted this to be right, you know? Not like this. But the thought of it just being sucked out. Men . . . they just don't know shit."

"Don't they?" Bobby put her hand on Sherry's arm. "Sort it out, girl. You've got to talk to him."

Sherry looked blankly into her empty glass while Bobby went in search of Sam. When she looked up, Rix was staring at her across the dance floor. She met his gaze and then curled her finger to call him over.

Rix jostled his way through the crowd until he stood in front of her.

"Look, baby. I'm sorry. I didn't mean to piss you off. I threw them away, honest."

Sherry's eyes started to well up with tears. She put her arms round Rix's neck, pulled his face close to hers and kissed him.

Bean had ducked down under the deck to do some exploring on his own. He didn't really like parties. He liked the music but too many people always made him feel small. Besides, when the others were having such a good time he didn't like to disturb them. Ducking through a small wooden hatch, he found himself in a long empty hall. Along one wall were hung various painted wooden figureheads. Sea captains, dragons and some bearded fellow who looked Captain Birdseye. Bean examined them one by one, toasting them with slugs of champagne. Right in the middle of the row, he came across a topless mermaid. He was captivated by her cheeky smile, flowing painted hair and generous wooden breasts. Especially their nipples, which jutted out towards him like hat pegs. He reached out tentatively and tweaked one between his thumb and forefinger.

"Why, madam, what large firm breasts you have," he said under his breath

"Thank you," said a voice behind him.

"Fuck!" Bean spun round, terrified.

A pretty brunette stood behind him. She fell about laughing as Bean clasped his chest in terror.

"Funny is it? Nearly shat myself . . . Fuck!"

"Sorry," said the girl, wiping tears of mirth from her big brown eyes.

"S'all right," said Bean.

"You going to drink all that by yourself?" she said, eyeing Bean's champagne bottle. She held out her champagne flute.

Bean poured some into her glass. "What you doing down here anyway?"

"Well . . ." she began. "Firstly I'm drunk and secondly I used to come here on school trips. I wanted to see if all this stuff was still here."

"Oh, right, me too."

She flicked her long fringe out of her eyes and plonked herself down on a bench that looked out over the cobbled square. She patted the seat next to her. Bean, a little surprised, sat down too.

Ten minutes later the bottle was nearly gone.

"What's your name by the way?" she asked.

"Bean."

"Really? Are you Bobby's mate?"

"Yeah, that's right," said Bean. "How'd you know?"

"I work with her. That's why I'm here. Some old queen came into the building society and when he saw Bobby, he invited us both."

Bean nodded.

"I'm Rachel, by the way." She held out her hand. Bean shook it formally.

"Good laugh, is it?"

"What?"

"Working with Bob."

"Oh yeah. Nine to five, five days a weeks. Lovely." She paused to take another huge slug of booze. "You're a musician, right?

"Yeah," said Bean, swelling with pride. "Sam's our manager. He's upstairs now. Might be getting us a deal."

"Oh yeah?"

"We might be famous one day."

"Sounds good."

"Would you like to be famous?"

"Oh, I dunno," said Rachel, thinking. "What are the hours?"

They both cracked up.

As she laughed her head dropped onto Bean's shoulder. She went quiet, feeling suddenly awkward. "Sorry."

"No problem."

On the deck above them, they heard a new band being announced on stage.

"My lords, ladies and gentlemen, South East Management give you the next big thing! Put your hands together for *Vibe Tribe*!" The crowd roared.

"Brilliant," said Rachel. "Down in one, eh?"

Rachel knocked back her glass in one swig. Bean tried to

58

follow but ended up choking. He coughed, spluttering out the champagne. A dribble of the fizz ran out of his nose, which he quickly wiped away on his shirt sleeve.

"Very cool, Bean," said Rachel with a wicked smile.

"Hate this stuff."

"Free is free."

"You ain't gonna ask me about my eye?"

"Is it a good story?"

"No."

"Then I'd prefer to dance." Rachel wobbled unsteadily to her feet and pulled Bean up by the scruff of his neck. "Shall we?"

"Yeah," said Bean, "that'd be wicked."

Sam was at the bar nursing a glass of champagne. He scanned the crowd for any useful record company people.

"All right, lover?" said Bobby. "Fancy a dance?"

"Not now, Bob, I'm working."

"You look like you're standing around like a spare prick to me, but then I don't know the record business like you do."

"Thanks for your support."

"You're the manager." Bobby beckoned to the barman to fill up her glass.

Sam spotted an old friend of his father's on the other side of the room. He wore a dark suit with an open-neck white shirt. He was speaking to a girl half his age. Sam moved towards him, only to bump shoulders with Elroy.

Elroy brushed off the shoulder of his jacket.

"In a hurry?" he asked.

Elroy had a girl with him. She wore a lot of jewellery and a crop top. She looked suitably spaced out. The girl sniffed delicately and wiped her nose with a napkin from the bar.

"Well, you certainly have gone up in the world, Elroy," said Sam, eyeing Elroy's companion

"This ain't school no more, little rich kid," he hissed. "This is the fucking real world. Where little people like you get hurt. You get me?"

Sam bristled.

Lucy, now high as a kite, staggered out of the crowd and tugged urgently at Sam's sleeve.

"Sam, have you seen Charlie?" she slurred. "I just went to the loo and he's *totally* disappeared!"

Elroy sucked his teeth and walked away. Sam looked at Lucy in disbelief.

"No, Luce, I haven't. I'm working, right?" As he spoke a Hawaiian shirt floated down out of sky and fluttered behind Lucy's head. "Oh no." said Sam.

Lucy's big eyes followed the shirt as it glided to the floor. In a moment of terrible realisation, they both retraced its path across the dance floor and up the main mast of the ship.

"Charlie!" Lucy shouted, clasping a hand to her mouth.

Sam winced at the volume of Lucy's scream. High up in the rigging sat Charlie, waving down at them with a huge smile. He was shirtless.

"Oh, my God," said Bobby, stunned.

Sam rubbed his forehead slowly. "Fucking great. This is all I need."

Charlie sat on the yardarm high above the party. He waved at revellers below, gallantly accepting the huge cheer which went up as they spotted him.

Bean was bopping shyly with Rachel on the dance floor when he heard the commotion. Seeing Charlie up the rigging, he gave him a big wave. Charlie beckoned him up. Bean, without thinking, headed for the rigging.

"Bean, no!" called Rachel.

Bean hoisted himself off the side of the boat and onto the rigging. He climbed quickly up to get some distance between himself and the fast-approaching bouncers. As he climbed he felt the eyes of the whole party on him. It felt great.

Charlie was waiting for him on the yardarm. Hanging over the edge to get a better view of Bean's upturned face, he took a couple of snaps with a pocket camera.

"What a great fucking picture."

"Fucking long way up for a snap shot," said Bean.

Charlie hauled his far from confident-looking friend up next to him.

"Ain't this great, Bean?" Charlie said.

"Yeah, Rachel's tits look even bigger from up here." Bean smirked and waved at Rachel.

"Eh?"

"Rachel. She works with Bobby in the building society."

Charlie gave Bean a long lingering look. "You sly dog." Charlie took a deep breath and looked around him at the twinkling lights of the city. "Check it out, man. Ain't it just the most . . ." Lost for words, Charlie threw his arms round Bean, almost toppling them both. "I love you, man."

"Love you too. Just don't kill me in the process," pleaded Bean, gripping the mast.

Charlie took a couple of casual pictures of the crowd below. By now the bouncers were making their way unsteadily up the rigging after them. Charlie snapped wildly. In every direction he could see miles of gleaming black water broken up by the reflected colours of the party. With a determined grin he climbed to his feet. Raising his arms in the air he shouted, "Top of the . . . fucking . . . world."

The crowd cheered again.

6

The telephone was ringing. Right by Sam's head. He stuck his arm unsteadily out of his duvet and pulled the receiver off its cradle.

"Yeah?" It was Henry.

"Let's just forget your friend's acrobatics last night, shall we?"

"Oh, Christ, I'm sorry."

"I wouldn't worry, darling, most people loved it. *Vibe Tribe* were a trifle pissed off at being upstaged, as you might imagine."

"Like I say, I'm really sorry."

"Your band. I've been listening to your tape. The snooker club, 3.30 today." He hung up. Sam blinked and checked the alarm clock by his bed: 11 am. "Shit!"

He moved to get out of bed. Bobby, who was draped over him under the covers, groaned.

"Don't go."

"I've got to get up."

"Hmm," said Bobby, feeling him under the covers. "Someone's already up."

"Leave it out, Bobby, This is serious." Sam slid out of bed and surveyed his room for any clean clothes he could grab easily.

Bobby sat up in bed and pulled the duvet up to her chin.

"You know, we hardly ever have time to make love any more."

"Bobby, not now."

"We used to be at it like rabbits."

"And we will again," said Sam, pulling on a dressing gown.

"When?"

"Look," said Sam. He sniffed a polo shirt then threw it back on the floor. "I just gotta sort this. Henry's heard the tape, he wants to talk." He paused to compose himself. "I'm doing this for you, you know."

"Yeah, well, I'd rather have a bit more of your sweet stuff."

"And you will . . ." said Sam. He leant over the bed and

kissed her on the nose. Bobby made a grab for him which he skilfully avoided. ". . . right after I've got the deal." He picked up the trousers he had worn the night before and went out the door.

Bobby threw herself back against her pillow and snuggled down into the duvet.

Sam padded downstairs with his trousers still in one hand. As he passed Charlie's room, he heard the rhythmic thumping of bed head against the wall. He stopped to listen at the door; smiling at the sound of friends' frenzied lovemaking. Lucy was screaming and moaning as Charlie was urging her on; repeating her name over and over.

"Christ!" said Sam and carried on down the stairs.

He stopped at a round window which looked out into his garden. He leant his face against the cool glass, balancing on it as he pulled on his trousers. As he struggled with his zip, he saw Bean and Rachel in varying states of undress asleep in a big Mexican hammock slung between two trees. A blanket lay over them as they slept.

"It's all going on," he said to himself.

"Come in me," pleaded Lucy as she ground herself onto Charlie's hips.

"What?" said Charlie, opening his eyes in panic.

"Come in me, please!" she demanded. She moved herself faster on top of him.

"Christ!" Charlie shoved her off. She landed heavily next to him on the bed, breathless and shiny with a thin sheen of sweat. "What was that all about?"

"Nothing," said Lucy. She pushed back a strand of hair which had stuck to her forehead and then swung her legs over Charlie so she sat up on the side of the bed. She swept her long blonde hair back into a bunch and held it with one hand, letting the morning air cool the flush off her cheeks.

Charlie moved round next to her and slipped his arms around her waist.

"Lucy, chill out. What's wrong?"

"Nothing."

"Luce."

"I, just . . ." She made to get up. Charlie grabbed her, hauling her back down onto the bed.

"It's nothing." Lucy smiled. "I love you, Charlie. I really do."

Rix and Sherry slept in a room next to Sam's. Sherry was awake. She lay with an arm stretched across Rix, watching him as his slept. Rix never snored but instead made a series of rhythmic grunts and mumbles all night long. Music even in his sleep she used to say. She ran her forefinger through the tight bush of curly hair in the middle of his chest. She wondered if her baby would look like him. A little Rix with tiny dreads and Fisher-Price turntables.

Rolling onto her back, she pulled up her nightie and ran her hand over her tummy. In her morning fug, Rix's breathing almost felt like her baby's. She knew then that Bobby was right. For better or worse she had to tell him.

"Rix," she whispered into his ear. "Rix. Get up, it's late."

Rix muttered.

"Rix?"

Rix shook his head lightly without regaining consciousness.

"I cut your dreads off last night." A grunt.

"Dyed your pubes blond." Another grunt.

"Rix." She put her lips right next to his ear. "I'm pregnant."

Rix made a noise like a muffled growl and rolled over onto his side. Looking at Rix's back, Sherry sighed. She got out of the bed, picked up one of his outsized T-shirts and slipped out of the room.

As the door clicked shut, Rix's eyes snapped open.

"What!" he roared.

Sophie, Sam's mum, was in the kitchen. She was an attractive widow, fifty years old, classically dressed and still stunning. As Sam entered she was rummaging in a cupboard. Next to her stood a smart-looking man in a blazer.

"What do you think about this one?" she said to her companion as she pulled a dusty bottle of red wine from a rack of such bottles in the cupboard.

The man took the bottle and squinted at the label, creasing his deeply tanned skin. He looked much younger than Sophie, probably no more than ten years older than Sam. He nodded indifferently.

"Hi, darling," she said as she spotted Sam at the door.

"Mum."

"You know Alfonso?"

Sam nodded at the man, who nodded back. Sophie put the bottle in a big wicker picnic basket which sat on the kitchen table.

"We're off for a picnic," she announced.

"Really?"

"There's some coffee for you over there." Sam went over to the percolator and filled a cup.

"See you later then," said Sophie, taking the man's arm. She stopped at the door and as an afterthought said, "How was Henry's party?"

"All right. He wants you to give him a call."

"That's nice. Actually, have you got any spare cash, darling?"

Sam pulled his wallet out of the pocket of his trousers and gave her a sheaf of notes.

"Thanks. Got to fly. Just stopped for a change of clothes." Sophie passed Bobby in the doorway. "Hi, Bobby!"

Bobby smiled.

Sam shook his head as he wandered over to the open French windows that led out into the garden.

"Unbelievable."

Sam stared vacantly at Bean and Rachel curled up in the hammock.

"I can't believe that girl likes Bean."

"Why not?" Bobby busied herself searching the cupboards for breakfast.

"Well, he's hardly Cary Grant, is he?"

Sherry stormed through the kitchen. She grabbed Sam's

coffee out of his hand as she passed before disappearing into the garden.

"Charming."

Rix's voice boomed down the hall after her.

"Sherry!" He burst into the kitchen, completely naked. "You ain't fucking keeping it!" He followed her into the garden.

Sam raised an eyebrow as Rix's firm buttocks disappeared across the lawn. He turned to Bobby.

"Is Sherry pregnant?" he asked idly. She nodded. "Whatever, I've got to get dressed."

Lucy was still perched on the edge of the bed as Charlie struggled to slip into his leathers.

"I know when something's wrong, Luce. Why don't you at least try to tell me."

"I dunno," she said. "I'm still working in the estate agent's and you're . . ." She paused. "You're going off to God knows where with God knows who."

Charlie stopped his struggles and put a warm arm across her shoulders.

"I ain't going nowhere. Least of all without you."

"You're about to be surrounded by all these beautiful women. Travel all over the world."

"You're jealous."

"I just don't want to lose you to some skinny, rich, beautiful tart."

"All right, I'll make sure she's fat, ugly and skint then."

Lucy smiled. She could never stay angry with Charlie for long. "Come on, I gotta go. I'll make you a cup of coffee."

Rix's naked tirade rang around the garden. It sheer volume shook Bean and Rachel awake. They popped their heads out from under their blanket to be confronted by Rix's naked form.

"Fuck mine," Bean whispered. Rachel giggled. Bean put his hand over her eyes in mock horror.

"Whether I keep it or not is up to me, Rix, not you!"

"Like fuck it is!"

"This is about me, Rix. What's happening inside me! Maybe I don't want your fucking kid anyway."

"Oh, I see. You trying to tell me this kid ain't even mine?"

"You ain't listening to me."

"You're talking crazy, Sherry. I mean, what about the band?"

"You selfish, fucking bastard! All I wanted was bit of support." Sherry turned and headed for the house.

"Sherry!"

Charlie and Lucy entered the kitchen just as Sherry was leaving it.

"You all right, Sherry?" Charlie asked as she whisked past him.

"No, I'm not. I'm fucking pregnant." She ran off down the corridor.

Charlie looked at Bobby and Sam, who smiled weakly, and then on to Rix, who stood naked and furious on the lawn. Bean and Rachel were still peering out from the hammock like a pair of startled owls.

"Oh, right," said Charlie as it all clicked into place. "Sherry's pregnant. Rix is naked. Bean's pulled for the first time in his life and it's my last day on wheels." He picked up his helmet and planted a sharp kiss on Lucy's cheek. "Sweet cheeks. I think I'll skip the coffee if you don't mind."

7

"21 . . . You got a pick up at Tottenham Court; drop at 41 Beak Street. 54 Whitfield wait and return from 10 Dorset Square. 37 North Hamilton Circle to Lansdowne Road. 19 Cologne to Overstrand Mansions 20 Queens Road to number 4 Curotham Road."

Henry struck the cue ball hard. It hit the triangle of red balls with a crack, scattering them across the smooth green baize of the snooker table.

"It's twenty years since I started coming to this place," he said grandly. "Your dad loved it here."

Sam looked around him at the dimly lit snooker hall. Its wood panelling had seen better days and its decor was straight out of *Oliver Twist*. An assortment of tough-looking characters sat around with cards or downed pints at the bar. All natural light had been blocked out in favour of the green glow of the long lamps over the tables.

"Certainly is an interesting place . . ." said Sam, stuffing his hands in his pockets.

"This place has seen some of the heaviest bastards south of the river." Henry lined up another shot.

"Yeah?" Sam laughed. "Wouldn't have thought it was your cup of tea."

"You just think I'm an old poof, don't you?" Henry said. He looked at Sam across the top of his cue.

"Well, it had crossed my mind," Sam said with a smile.

Henry's face remained impassive. He was dressed smartly in moleskin trousers and matching waistcoat; his jacket was slung causally across the back of a chair. His balding head and world-weary face suited the dark mood of the snooker club. Henry straightened up, planting the base of cue at his feet.

"Come 'ere, Sam," he said with an air of menace.

Sam walked round the polished wood edge of the snooker table until he stood in front of Henry. Like lightning Henry wrapped his free arm tight round Sam's neck and whispered in his ear. "I'm warning you, boy. Don't fuck with me." He released Sam, who staggered slightly with shock.

"What?"

Henry pointed his finger into Sam's face. "I promised your dad I'd look after you. And I have. Like you were my own. But bear this in mind, I am also the executor of his will, so you be a bit more fucking careful what you say around me."

"What the fuck have I done?"

"Fuck all! That's the point. Your becoming a trustafarian, Sam."

"What's that?"

"A wanker who lives off his daddy's money."

Sam was taken aback. "Look, I loved my dad, but you and I both know he was a selfish cunt. He was so busy making money, he was never there when I needed him."

"Selfish!" Henry slammed his cue flat on the corner of the table. "He was a barrow boy, for fuck's sake! Who turned himself into a millionaire. He wanted you to have all the things he never did . . . Your father worked himself to death for you. He was being eaten up from inside but he was still grafting twelve hours a day to put food on the table and a roof over your head for life . . . And how have you repaid him, eh?"

"I'm trying with the band . . ."

"Bollocks. Where'd you get the bottle to call yourself a manager? Going around telling my contacts that you've got a vocalist that don't even exist."

"Oh, come on, Henry! Don't be a mean bastard! I was just fucking about."

"You want to fuck about? Do it in the playground. Don't embarrass me in front of my business associates."

Henry calmed himself. He pulled his waistcoat straight and bent over the table to pot another red.

"Jesus," said Sam. He ran his fingers through his hair.

"Your father and I made a fortune because we were hungry and nothing could stop us," Henry continued. "Can you say the same thing about yourself?"

Sam looked around the snooker hall to see if anyone had noticed Henry's outburst.

"Henry, I . . ."

Henry held up a hand to stop him. "You better think about it, boy. Now fuck off."

"21 . . . 21 . . . You at Whitfield Street yet? Get a fucking move on! I got Dorset Square giving me fucking earhole. You got 37 North Hamilton Circle to Lansdowne Road. 19 Cologne Road and Queens Road. Today. You hear me, 21? You want your fucking cheque you better get your finger out of your fucking arse!"

Bean and Rachel were stretched out on two inflatable beds. As they floated gently across Sam's swimming pool they orbited each other slowly, keeping in touch with the tips of their fingers. Bean had his head on one side so he could look at Rachel, his mind swimming after their night together. Rachel wore a baggy borrowed swimsuit and was hidden under a huge pair of plastic sunglasses. Beneath them he could see her eyes were closed as she smiled up into the afternoon sun. Bean had never seen anyone look so beautiful.

"Close your eyes. You could be anywhere. On a sandy beach with crystal blue waters. Maybe Barbados. Maybe Bali. Wouldn't that be great?"

"Yeah," said Bean.

He shifted onto his back to look up at the sky, trying to stretch his imagination to follow Rachel's dreams.

"Always wanted to get as far away from this place as possible," she continued. "Still do. Get away from my family, my job and all the rest of that shit. Just jump on a plane and never come back." Rachel took off her sunglasses and looked at him. "If you could go anywhere, absolutely anywhere, where would you go," she asked.

"Never been abroad," said Bean.

"Never?"

"Never even seen the sea."

"You're kidding! Your parents never took you to the sea-side."

"Mum died."

"I'm sorry, Bean."

"'S nuffin." He rolled sideways into the pool. He emerged right next to her, their faces were inches apart. "I know where I'd like to go."

"Where?"

"Ireland. County Kerry. Mum's ashes are scattered on a beach there."

"What's it like?"

"I saw it in a picture once. It's beautiful. Really calm." Bean paused to pluck up courage. "Would you go to Ireland with me?"

Rachel looked into his eyes. "Yeah, I would."

Bean smiled. "You would?"

Rachel nodded.

"I better tell Sam to get us some money together then."

"Tell you what. When I win the lottery I'll go to Ireland and I'll take you with me. We all need a little escape." Rachel winked at him.

Rix, now dressed but still grim with anger, emerged from the garage.

"Bean!" he shouted. "Are we gonna play some music today or what?"

Bean nodded over to the garage.

"You don't always need a plane to escape, Rachel."

"21 . . . Where are you, 21 . . . because I'm about to tear your cheque in half, I got pick-ups at Tower Bridge and Moorgate. Are you receiving me, 21? Cologne Road and Queens Road. Those names mean anything to you? Are you deaf?"

Rix was connecting a cable to the back of his mixing desk with a small screwdriver when Bean finally pulled Rachel into the garage.

"At last," said Rix.

"Look I don't want to disturb you guys," said Rachel.

72

Bean sat her down in a deck chair and picked his trumpet out of its open box. He was bursting with excitement.

"Okay," said Rix, taking position behind the desk. "What are we gonna do?"

"Anything," said Bean.

"Anything?" Rix raised an eyebrow.

Bean nodded eagerly.

"Anything it is."

Rix put on his headphones. He flicked a series of switches and slowly faded the music in. A sweeping flat electronic sound that filled the room like an approaching storm. Deep within it were the muffled sounds of city life: car horns, sirens and babies crying. Rix punctuated this soundscape with tiny scratches from his decks. He built the atmosphere until it was overpowering. Then he dropped in a jungle beat of urgent bass and super-fast high hat. Rachel looked around her, impressed by how good the sound was. Bean, with his eyes still locked on her, put his trumpet to his lips and played.

"Fuck mine," whispered Rix. The sound was sweeter than anything Rix had heard him play before. Higher and clearer; shot through with a strength and optimism that were totally new. Rix, momentarily stunned, watched Bean as his music came alive. He tilted his body and screwed up his eyes, straining to squeeze every last note from the horn. It was a haunting and passionate melody that could reach right down into your soul. Bean's song rose high above the backing track until his trumpet was all you could hear. It was a music that conjured images and feelings in the imagination. Intertwined scales that raised the intensity of the piece to an incredible climax. Then just as soon as he'd begun, the song ended. Silence surged into the vacuum.

Bean lowered the trumpet from his lips nervously. Rachel was stunned. Without thinking she stood and kissed Bean hard on his warm lips. Rix, equally surprised, pulled off his headphones and rubbed his ears.

"Bean, mate, whatever you're taking, you gotta get me some."

Bean gave him a grin.

"21, you useless cunt. I want you at Queens Road in fifteen minutes or you can forget your fucking cheque. You hear me, 21? I don't care if you get a ticket. I don't care if you end up under a fucking juggernaut. Just get there!"

Charlie dropped a gear and banked down hard as he approached the corner. Leaning into the road, he felt the G force hold him. He pulled the accelerator back let the bike jump ahead, pulling him out of the turn. Ahead of him, the dirty back doors of a white transit were coming up fast. He eased off the gas and tucked the bike into its slipstream. There was something written with a finger in the grime. He moved closer to read it.

"Don't clean me, plant potatoes."

Charlie laughed. He flicked his indicator and pulled out sharply, gunning the engine with hoarse roar. He didn't see the van's red brake lights come on, but he did see the car pulling out in front of him. He was wide-eyed as he hit the brakes. He felt his back wheel slide out from under him like the bike was bending in two. The engine went dead. There was the sound of crushed metal and he was flying.

"21, I've got your cheque in my hand and I'm tearing it up. You're done, you cunt. It's over."

"Thanks for a totally great night," said Rachel.

The same battered Mondeo minicab, this time without its mate, pulled up at the end of Sam's drive.

"Can I see you again?" said Bean.

Rachel kissed him on the cheek. "Of course. You've got my number. We've got to work out how we're going to get the money together to get to Ireland." Rachel walked down the drive and opened the back door of the car. She stopped and blew Bean a kiss before she climbed in.

Bean watched the car pull away. He watched it drive all the

way down Sam's road until it finally disappeared around a corner.

"You shagged her yet?" said Ani, who had appeared by his side.

"Christ, Ani. You're only six."

"Nearly seven," she said proudly.

The sound of the telephone shook Bean out of his spell. He closed the front door and went through to the living room. Rix and Sherry sat next to each other on the sofa with their arms folded. They glared silently at the TV. On the table next to them, the telephone rang.

"Get the bloody phone, will you?" said Rix.

"Get it yourself!"

Bean frowned. It put his perfect weekend with Rachel in perspective. Ani ran past him and picked up the phone.

"Hello, Sam's house," she said. She listened for a while to the voice at the other end. Her smile faded. "It's Lucy," she said, "and she's crying."

8

At the hospital, Rix, Bean and Sherry were ushered by a nurse into a small white waiting room. The laminated sign on the door read "Family Room". It was empty except for a couple of wooden chairs and a low table with some yellowing magazines stacked on it. A wide window looked out over the hospital car park. Lucy sat chewing at her nails In one corner, next to her were Mr and Mrs Rowntree, Charlie's parents. His mum held Lucy's hand and blew her nose into a tissue with the other. His dad sat stiffly beside his wife with his arm over her shoulders. As they entered, Lucy jumped up and ran towards them. Her eyes were swollen and red from crying. As Sherry embraced her, she started to weep again.

"Oh, God. What am I going to do?" she said into Sherry's shoulder. "I love him so much."

Rix shook hands with Mr Rowntree.

"How is he?"

"They brought him here in the air ambulance. Then they took him straight into surgery. There was an accident this afternoon. A van and two cars. That's all we know."

Bean looked with concern at Mrs Rowntree.

"Thank you for coming, Bean," she said. Her voice was weak and cracked.

"Came as soon as Lucy called." Bean sat down next to Charlie's mum. Bean spoke gently. "Is he? You know . . ."

When Mrs Rowntree didn't answer, Bean looked up at Charlie's dad. He shook his head.

A nurse in green overalls entered.

"Good news. Your son is out of theatre and into intensive care."

"What sort of condition is he in?" said Charlie's dad.

"The doctor will be here soon to answer all your questions."

Lucy pushed past Sherry.

"I want to see him," she said.

Charlie's mum put a hand on her shoulder to calm her.

"We'd all like to see him, love. Let's just let the doctors do their job." She thanked the nurse.

"Please, the doctor will be here soon." The nurse disappeared out of the door again.

For half an hour they sat in silence. Trying to take in why they were there and the events of that afternoon. Bean took a whip-round for small change and fetched coffee from a machine in the hall. Periodically Sherry lit up a cigarette, only to stub it out angrily when Rix silently pointed at the "No Smoking" sign on the wall. They shifted position uneasily on the thin padding of their seats.

The slapping sound of running in the corridor announced the others. Sam was breathless as he entered, his car keys still in his hand. He wiped the sweat off his forehead and scanned their faces for any sign of what was happening.

"Where is he?" he said to Rix. "Can we see him?"

Rix shook his head. Bobby went to Lucy and knelt beside her, holding her hands. Sam, realising that nothing could be done, slumped into a chair exhausted.

Another hour went past. They took turns to stretch their legs and to look out of the window at the darkening evening sky. Sam flicked through magazines. He barely focused on the articles, whipping the pages across his lap as he turned them.

Finally, a young doctor in a white coat joined them. He held a clipboard and had a stethoscope hanging in a lazy loop from one pocket.

"Mr and Mrs Rowntree?" he asked. Sam's parents looked up and nodded. "Your son is out of danger now, but due to the severity of his injuries he'll have to be transferred to Stoke Mandeville Spinal Unit."

"Can we see him?" asked Charlie's mum.

The doctor looked sympathetic. The dark rings of sleeplessness under his eyes softened. "Of course." He paused. "Please be aware that your son has had a very severe trauma. He is being helped by a life support machine and we have him in halo-traction to keep his spine straight. It can be quite a shock when you first see a loved one in this condition."

Charlie's mum nodded again uneasily and pressed her hanky over her mouth.

"If you'd like to come with me, I'll take you to him."

Charlie parents got to their feet slowly. Charlie's mum gripped her husband's arm so tightly it crumpled the tweed of his jacket. She took Lucy's forearm with the other. The doctor held the door open for them as they filed through.

"When can we see him?" asked Rix.

"It would be best to come back tomorrow. We'd prefer immediate family only. He really needs rest now, especially if we're going to move him."

Charlie's parents and Lucy locked themselves in a huddle. The doctor helped them down the hall.

There was a stunned silence in the room after they left. Then Sam clapped his hands together and chirped, "Right, back here tomorrow then." His voice was strangely brisk and cheery. The others looked at him puzzled. Sam seemed not to detect their surprise. He rubbed his hands together vigorously. "Who needs a lift? Bob?"

"I'll wait for Lucy," she said.

"Rix?"

"Got the van outside."

Sam looked at Bean expectantly. Bean shrugged.

"Suit yourselves. Tomorrow then." He strode out of the room.

The next day the family room felt strangely familiar to them after the hours they had spent there. The early morning sun illuminated a pattern of children's fingerprints on the lower half of the window. Only the magazines, which had been straightened, gave any indication of the six hours of troubled sleep that lay between their two visits.

The doctor, who had taken Charlie's parents and Lucy down the hall the night before, appeared in the doorway again.

"Bloody hell," said Sam. "You saving up for a car or something?"

The doctor smiled. "Double shift," he said. "I can take you through now."

79

They followed the doctor out of the family room and down a long gloomy corridor lined with the little square windows. Their footsteps were almost inaudible on its linoleum floor. They passed closed doors to other wards and the deserted detritus of medical operations: wheelchairs, trays of plastic cups and big laundry bins. At the end of the corridor the doctor stopped in front of a pair of thick plastic swing doors. A sign above them read "I.C.U. Authorised Personnel Only".

"As I warned you yesterday, intensive care can be a bit of shock . . ." the doctor began.

"That's all right, doc" said Sam, shifting uneasily. "We saw worse in 'Nam."

The doctor gave him a look. "Okay." He pushed one of the heavy doors open and ushered them in.

Intensive care was a dull blue colour. All the lights were on and with no windows it was hard to tell if it was night or day. The ward was quiet and the air felt hot and uncomfortably still. In the distance they heard the odd clicks and wheezes of machinery. Ahead of them there were the ends of four beds, each divided by the straight-edged nylon of hospital curtains.

A nurse sat at a desk by the door. She smiled and gestured for them to follow her. As they moved deeper into the room they saw they were not alone. A woman sat, knitting, in a silent vigil next to her comatose husband. An overweight man was propped up in the next bed drifting in a shallow sleep. There was a huge red gash down his chest where it had been slit to fit a pacemaker. As they approached the last bed in the room the mechanical noises became louder.

There was Lucy slumped in a chair by Charlie's bed.

She leant forward to clasp his hand between hers. They rounded the final curtain and she saw them. Shaking her head, she got up, put her hand over her mouth to stop herself wailing and ran from the room. Bobby went after her. Charlie was laid out straight on the bed and covered to the waist with a light blue counterpane. His bed stood between two huge banks of assembled machinery: boxes fronted with dials and knobs and rows of digital readouts which danced to the tune of his heartbeat.

The machinery was connected to his prone body by a network of wires and tubes. Some ran from the machines straight under the exposed skin of his arms, puncturing his flesh with needles held in place with transparent surgical tape. Others attached themselves to his torso with adhesive pads.

Charlie's spine was held rigid by a brutal iron crown, the halo-traction. It was attached to his head with a ring of stainless-steel bolts that extended from the crown and ended in bloody stumps screwed directly into the skull. The halo-traction pulled his neck and shoulders taut, imprisoning them in a rigid steel cage.

Charlie was immobile under the weight of the equipment. His eyes stared upwards to the ceiling, darting from side to side with silent pain. A hole had been dug in his throat for a tracheotomy tube. It's valve stuck straight out from his neck as if gasping for air itself. A ribbed tube was connected to the valve. It trailed across his body, finally fixing itself to the wheezing bellows which rhythmically pumped air into his lungs. The nurse leaned delicately over Charlie so he could see her.

"Your friends are here," she whispered.

Rix approached Charlie first. His throat was dry as he sat in the seat vacated by Lucy.

"All right, mate?" he said.

Behind him Bean stopped dead in his tracks, unsure whether to vomit or run screaming out of the ward and away from this terrible nightmare.

"What do you think of my new hat?" said Charlie. His voice was weak. What they could hear whistled and buzzed through his tracheotomy tube.

"Nah, don't think it'll catch on." Rix stared at the medieval brutality of the construction which held Charlie's head. "Too tricky to get on and off."

"I'm urgent for a cup of tea" croaked Charlie. The words were almost inaudible and seemed to come from within the machinery itself. As Charlie spoke its lights flickered and liquid dripped from tubes in his arms into waiting glass jars which hung from wire frames above him.

"Urgent for what?" said Rix looking around him.

"Tea," said the nurse. "He said, tea."

Sam stood at the end of Charlie's bed in deep shock. He thought he would cope better than this. He had spent hours in this very hospital watching his dad die after all. The tubes and the jars, the pills and the pain. The amazing shit that comes out of a body when it's sick. It was happening again.

"I made it last time," he said sharply. He wrapped his fingers round the cold metal end of Charlie's bed to steady himself. Charlie's cracked lips moved again.

"Is that Sam? Where is Sam?" Charlie's blue eyes darted again, trying to catch a glimpse of his friend.

"He's right here, mate, and Bean too," said Rix.

"Hello, Bean," said Charlie. He tried to smile.

Bean whimpered.

"Nice equipment, Geezer," said Sam as he surveyed the mass of wires and pipes. "Don't suppose you've got *Virtual Fighter 2* have you?"

"No, but the geezer next to me has."

Sam felt his chest tighten. The sickening movement of the bellows turned his stomach. He took a deep breath.

"You don't fuck about, mate. You always go the whole hog."

"You know me. Nothing by halves." Charlie screwed his eyes shut in agony.

"They tell you anything?"

"About what?" said Rix.

"About my neck." Charlie coughed. As his chest shook weakly small bubbles of phlegm swelled from the tracheotomy valve. The nurse moved quickly to remove the plastic pipe and insert a second tube deep into Charlie's neck. The second tube sucked the phlegm from his throat with a grotesque gurgle. Charlie closed his eyes.

No one noticed Bean. His face was sheet white and his eyes had rolled up into his head. He swayed behind Rix as if performing some exotic snake-charming dance before tipping backwards as he lost consciousness. He landed on the ground with a heavy thump. The nurse calmly reinserted the tracheotomy valve and walked round the bed to Bean's prostrate body.

"What happened?" said Charlie, scared and powerless.

Rix looked behind him at Bean's crumpled body. "It's Bean," said Rix as he turned back to Charlie. "He's only fucking fainted." Rix smiled warmly at Charlie. "A bit of comic relief, eh?"

Sam looked down at Bean from the end of the bed. He stood like a man balanced on the edge of a precipice unable to move to help him. He gripped the bed end as if fighting a high wind. He was sweating. His mind raced, images of his father mixing with those around him. "Just remembered I owe you twenty quid," he blurted. He blinked as he spoke, trying to shut out the machines if only for a second.

The nurse helped Bean to his feet and gently dusted down his front. "Sit down. I'll get you a glass of water."

"Want to sit near my mate," said Bean.

Rix stood up so Bean could sit down next to Charlie.

"Hello, mate," said Charlie. Bean's eyes filled with tears. Charlie thought for a second. "I can't feel . . ."

"Eh?" said Bean.

"I can't feel anything."

The nurse, sensing trouble, touched Bean on the shoulder.

"You'd all best go. He needs his rest. They're moving him tomorrow."

"I must look pretty scary," said Charlie, trying to lighten the mood with a smile. No one laughed. "Don't go."

"We have to," said Rix. "We'll see you tomorrow, mate."

Charlie's smile faded.

"Rix, I can't feel anything. . ." He was desperate. "What am I going to do? Bean, oh fuck! Help me!"

"It's early days yet, mate," said Rix. His voice was strong and calm. "See what happens. We'll sort it out." He looked at Sam and Bean. "We'll get through it together."

Sam flushed and strode towards the exit.

Behind him, Rix followed slowly as he gathered his thoughts.

Bean stayed in his chair and looked quizzically at his crippled friend. Charlie's tears were drying on his cheeks. The nurse dabbed them off with a tissue.

"You calm down now, love," she said.

Charlie blinked back some more.

Bean stood as if to join the others. Then almost as an afterthought, he bent slowly over and, lifting Charlie's hand to his lips, kissed his friend goodbye.

Sam burst through the plastic doors. He was panting and breathless as if a heavy weight had been dropped on his chest. In the corridor he leant back on the cool painted plaster of the wall. He tipped back his head, tapping it against the smooth surface behind him to jar the images of Charlie out of his mind. Rix emerged from the I.C.U. stunned. He rubbed his hand slowly across his face before he noticed Sam.

"You all right, Sam?" he asked. Panic seized Sam. His mind felt blank, all he knew was that he had to get out of the hospital fast. The feel of its sickness and despair was seeping through his clothes, consuming him.

"Mate?" said Rix.

"I've gotta go," said Sam. "Got an appointment. Important stuff about the band."

"I think that can wait a bit, mate," said Rix. "We got to discuss what we do about Charlie." But Sam was already running down the corridor.

"Sorry. Got to go. Meeting," he called over his shoulder. He passed Bobby coming down the corridor carrying two plastic coffee cups. He went straight on without stopping.

"Sam!"

Bean emerged from the plastic doors.

"What's up with Sam?"

"I dunno, mate," said Rix. "I really don't."

After the hospital Bean went home. He didn't feel right going to Charlie's, not now he wouldn't be back.

Upstairs in his room he broke down and cried. Forcing his face into his pillow to deaden the noise. Apart from his own mother, Charlie was the only person who'd ever cared about Bean. Even when Lucy had come along he'd always had time for him. Bean felt very alone.

Then he remembered Rachel. He reached into his jeans pocket and pulled out a small square of paper, then picked up the phone.

The phone rang twice before someone picked it up.

"Yeah?" said a gruff man's voice. Bean was confused. He had not expected a man to answer. He looked at the crumpled piece of paper in his hand. The number he had called was written in round girlish handwriting underneath the name Rachel and a little love heart.

"Is this 536 3321?" Bean said.

"Yeah."

"Is Rachel there?"

"She might be," said the voice. "Who wants to know?"

"Never mind . . ." Bean hung up. He looked again at the piece of paper in his hand. Maybe she had a flatmate, he thought. He neatly folded the paper into quarters and tucked it behind a picture of Miles Davis which was fixed with Blu-Tack to the wall above his bed.

Downstairs he could hear the muffled noise of the TV. Brian and his cronies were back from the pub; they were shouting and moving around the living room clumsily in their drunkenness. Outside the rain poured down. The night was so dark you could barely see the sombre grey corners of the estate. Some of tower blocks almost looked romantic in this weather, like distant mountains rather than ugly monsters.

He reached for his trumpet, which stood upright on the window-sill. As he put the instrument to his lips a particularly loud shout echoed up from downstairs. Bean thought twice about playing. Instead he hugged the horn to his chest and curled up on his bed to watch the rain.

"Who was that on the phone?" called Rachel. She leant out from the bathroom. She wore a heavy towelling robe and had her head cocked to one side as she dryed off her hair with a hairdryer.

Chris, Rachel's ex, was slumped on her sofa watching TV.

"Dunno," he said.

Rachel clicked off the dryer. Furious, she padded out from the bathroom in her bare feet until she stood between Chris and the TV.

"Don't answer my phone any more. You don't live here any more, remember! Now who was it?" Chris leant to one side so he could see past her.

"Wrong number."

Rachel let out a shriek of exasperation.

"You're only staying until you find a place. Don't make yourself at home." She stormed back into the bathroom and slammed the door.

Chris shrugged and sunk deeper into the sofa.

Charlie was asleep at last, his desperate eyes finally subdued by morphine. Lucy sat and watched him. When he was asleep you could almost forget the machines that stopped her from hugging him. He seemed normal when he slept, as if he was just hiding under the iron crown and any second would come round with a wink and a cheery "Hello, sweet cheeks". Beside her Bobby snored quietly, her arm hung over the back of her chair, cradling her head. In her lap a half-drunk cup of coffee was slowly sliding towards the floor. Lucy delicately lifted it from between her legs. As she bent over to put the cup on the floor she heard Charlie make a little snuffling noise. She had heard that noise often in the many nights they had spent together.

Bent under the bed in the darkness, she listened to him sleep and smiled with happy memories.

"Lucy?" said a woman's voice. Lucy sat up to see a nurse. She was carrying a white plastic bag. "Mrs Rowntree signed for these. Can you make sure she gets them?"

"Sure," said Lucy.

When the nurse had gone she opened the bag. It contained Charlie's possessions taken from him after the crash. His wallet, a lighter, and a broken camera in among his familiar biking gear. She also saw something that always made her smile. Reaching into the bag she pulled out Charlie's wristwatch. She had given it to him for his birthday two years ago. A Mickey Mouse watch. She had bought it because Mickey's expression was so goofy it reminded her immediately of Charlie. The watch had stopped now; it's glass face was broken. As she touched Mickey's frail tin arms through the shattered glass she knew he would never move again.

After the hospital, Rix just walked. He made his way through the streets with his shoulders hunched and his hands buried deep in the pockets of his overcoat. He thought about Charlie; about what he was and what he would never be again. The man who climbed masts, rode trains and whose noisy sounds of shagging had kept them all awake. He wondered how his friend would live and he wondered how he himself would feel about never kicking a ball his way again. By the time he got to Greenwich Common it had started to rain. Rix sat on a wet bench and stared through the night. The night was black now and the city was just a blanket of light; like the sky had fallen down and his whole world was upside down.

Rix thought about Sherry. It confused him that he could see a future for Charlie but none for himself if it didn't include her. Before long he was walking again. Wondering about his kid and what kind of footballer he was going to be. As daybreak came he found himself outside Sherry's door.

He rang the bell.

After a while a light came on in the hall and the door opened. It was Sherry. She looked sleepy and was wearing an oversized T-shirt. She rubbed her eyes as she looked the sodden Rix up and down.

"Who is it?" said a voice from behind her.

"It's okay," said Sherry.

Rix was drenched. His coat shone with water and his dreads hung heavily across his shoulders.

"I want us to keep it," he said.

Sherry's eyes began to mist up with tears.

"Rix, it's a terrible thing what happened to Charlie but it doesn't change anything . . ."

"It's not just Charlie," interrupted Rix. "I love you, Sherry. I want you in my life. I want both of you in my life."

Sherry stepped out into the rain and stood before Rix. He took her into his arms.

Sam took a final drag on his cigarette and sat down at the kitchen table. He stubbed out the butt in an ashtray which already contained a dozen others. A folder sat on the table in front of him. The same folder he had taken to the *Cutty Sark* a few nights previously. He pulled out the contact sheets from Charlie's photo shoot of the band and spread them out on the table top. He arranged the rows and rows of tiny Rixs, Beans and Bobbys in front of him. They were like all Charlie's photographs: they fizzled with life, passionate movement and intense shades. That was Charlie.

Sam shook his head. He reached into the folder again and brought out one final photograph. It was of him and Charlie. They had taken it with a self-timer. In the picture, they stood close with their arms tight around each other's necks; they both wore sunglasses and had joints hanging from their lips. Together they had their arms and fingers extended to flip the camera a resolute bird.

"You all right, darling?" Sam snapped out of his daze. It was his mum in her dressing gown. She had wandered in so quietly he hadn't heard her. She carried an empty glass in one hand. There was a newspaper tucked under her arm.

"Yeah, fine," said Sam as he stuffed the photograph of Charlie back into the folder and began to collect up the contact sheets. "Just doing a little work."

She pulled open the fridge and refilled her glass from a carton of orange juice. "Just like your father."

Sam got up from the table. "I'm off out."

"Nothing I said I hope."

"No."

"Okay, darling. Don't work too hard."

★

Bean had been waiting outside the building society since 7.30 that morning. He'd hadn't meant to get there that early but he couldn't sleep with Brian's snoring thundering through the wall next to him. He sat on a low wall on the opposite side of the road, swigging from a can of Coca-Cola. Having decided the night before that Rachel must have given him the wrong number by mistake, he had decided to come to the building society and wait for her.

All around him, the high street was waking up. Newsagents opened, cafés filled up with builders and the road slowly came to a halt as it packed out with cars driven by suited business-men or harassed mums on school runs.

He had just about given up when across the road he saw a car pull up next to the building society. Rachel sat in the passenger street.

Bean hopped off the wall and brushed off the back of his jeans. Then he saw that Rachel was not in the car alone.

"So," said Chris, turning to face Rachel, "you going to let me stay just a couple more days?"

Rachel looked at him impassively. "I told you no."

Chris leant across fast and kissed her, pinning her head back against her seat. She struggled underneath him before she finally shoved him off.

"C'mon, you don't mean that," said Chris with a guilty smirk.

"Yes, I fucking do. You take your stuff and get out." Rachel opened her door and climbed out. She leant back into the car. "If you're still there when I get home tonight, I'm going to call the police. Now fuck off." She slammed the car door. Rachel wiped her mouth on the sleeve of her jacket. "Fucking arsehole," she hissed under her breath.

Bean watched from the other side of the road as a manager unlocked the door for Rachel and she disappeared in through its thick glass doors. He couldn't believe what had happened. Rachel with some other man. He had nothing left, his whole world was gone.

Suddenly paranoid, he looked up and down the street to

see if anyone had seen what a prat he'd made of himself. As the tears began filling up his eyes, he turned and walked back down the street. His walk turned to a jog. By the time he had put a hundred yards between himself and the building society he was running fast, as fast, as he could away from Rachel.

Henry's secretary had known Sam since he was a kid. He used to play there when his dad was alive. She nodded him through to Henry's office without taking the telephone receiver from her ear. Henry office was huge. It was panelled with pale oak and had a wall of floor-to-ceiling windows which looked out across the river. It was decorated with fashionable designer furniture and abstract paintings. Henry himself sat behind a glass desk the size of a double bed, leaning back in a overstuffed leather chair. Behind him was an arrangement of gold and silver discs. He was shouting into the phone.

"My boys close the show or they don't fucking play." He waved at Sam. Sam positioned himself on a big leather sofa that ran along one wall. "Oh really. Well, when you learn to speak English, you call me back. All right?" He hung up the phone. "Sam, your mum called me. I heard about Charlie. Are you all right?"

"Yeah. But I'm not the one with bolts in my head and a road rash across my arse."

Henry frowned. He got up and walked over to a glass drinks cabinet. He got down two glasses and a bottle of Scotch.

"It's funny." Sam said. "Two days ago, I watched him ride off to work. I stood there and I thought, you good-looking talented fucker. I'd never really thought about it before."

Henry handed him a glass. "I know how you must feel."

"Good, because I fucking don't." Sam took a swallow of whisky. "Anyway I'm not here to talk about Charlie. You said I fuck about, been given it all on a plate. Well, not any more, I'm ready for change. I'm dead fucking serious about the band, Henry. I want to make them happen."

"You sure you want to talk about this now?" said Henry.

"I know the band have got a fucking wicked sound. It's one in a million."

"Easy, Sam. Your best mate is lying in hospital with a broken neck . . ."

Sam jumped up to face Henry; his eyes blazed. "You want me to cut a vein for Charlie. Is that it? There's nothing I can do for him. Nothing!" Sam took a deep breath. "It's what you do that counts, not what you say. You told me that."

Henry was taken aback. "Yes, but sweetheart . . ."

"So I'm ready. No more talk, no more fucking about." Henry looked in to his nephew's eyes. "And no more hand-outs. This is a business proposition. I'll give you a finder's fee and 10 per cent of the first money I make. All I need is a bit of advice, a desk and a telephone. Deal?"

Henry looked Sam up and down. He was impressed. "Deal," he said quietly.

"Right," said Sam. "You said we need a vocalist."

Henry nodded. He walked over to his desk and sorted through a pile of tapes. He picked out one and tossed it to Sam.

"Listen to this. Her name is Iona. Black and very beautiful. Deep, sexy voice. But she's got a serious ego . . . a real handful." Sam looked at the tape. "Have a listen. Then we'll talk."

"Thanks." Sam put down his glass and stood up. He turned to go but stopped. Weighing the tape up in his hand, he said, "You won't regret this, Henry. I promise."

When Sam got back to the house, the others were in the sitting room. The mood was sombre. Cigarettes burnt untouched in ashtrays and the TV was off. Bean was staring aimlessly out the window at a deserted lilo which floated in the middle of Sam's pool. That afternoon Bobby lay on one sofa. She had brought Lucy back from the hospital for the first time since the accident. Rix and Sherry had forced her to take a shower and change her clothes. Now they sat together on the other side of the room. Sherry brushed her hair as Lucy explained to them what the doctors had told her about Charlie's injuries. She spoke with the slow drawl of exhaustion.

"What the fuck's a C6?" said Rix.

"It's a vertebra. They go from one to eight up your neck. All the nerves and stuff that control your body are connected to there. The nurse said if you break C6 it's bad," said Lucy.

"Bad? How bad?"

"They're not sure."

"You mean they won't say," said Sherry.

"What! You mean, no one's told him he's likely to be paralysed from the neck down," said Rix.

Lucy nodded. It was Bobby who spoke from the other side of the room: "You want to tell him, big guy. Be my guest."

Sam spoke tentatively to test the water. "But Stoke Mandeville's the best place, is it?"

Everyone looked up.

"Where have you been," asked Bobby.

Sam let his body sink down into an armchair. "I mean, he's getting the best care, right?" he continued, ignoring her.

"Doctor says there's none better," said Lucy flatly.

"Okay, that's good."

"But there's little chance he'll recover."

"Well? Where *have* you been?" said Bobby.

"Talking to Henry," Sam said. "Doing some thinking."

"What kind of thinking," said Rix.

"Look." Sam leant forward. "I know this isn't the best time but Henry says we need a vocalist . . ."

Bean spoke, his stare still fixed on the water: "Well, he's wrong. We don't."

Sam sniffed with indignant irritation. "He's wrong is he? Then how comes he's rich and you're skint, eh?"

"Don't listen to him, Bean," said Bobby, shooting Sam a dirty look.

Bean wasn't. "I saw Rachel this morning."

Bobby looked surprised. "Oh yeah?"

"She was with someone. She kissed him. I couldn't believe it."

"Aw, Bean." Bobby went over to him and put her hand on his shoulder.

"I don't believe this," said Sam.

"Maybe this isn't the best time to discuss the band, Sam," said Bobby.

"Why? Because of him." Sam shook his head. "He's a sad wanker . . . Our mate is lying in hospital all fucked up and all he can think about is that. Some tart."

"Stop it, Sam," warned Bobby. "Leave him alone."

Sam frowned and sat back in his chair. He turned to Rix.

"We've got to move on this one, Rix. At least listen to a few of them, then make your mind up . . ."

Bean turned sharply from the window.

"Our mind is made up, isn't it, Rix?"

"Right now, my mind is shit."

"At least think about it, yeah?" urged Sam.

"There nothing to think about," shouted Bean. "Jazz jungle. We've got a unique sound. Who wants to play back-up for some bird who thinks singing is sucking a microphone?"

"What the fuck do you know?" said Sam.

"I know we don't need a vocalist."

Sam was on feet, his eyes burning into Bean. "Yeah? Who made you the expert? You who couldn't even look at Charlie in the hospital . . . You don't even know how to keep a girl."

Bean looked down at the ground, overcome with misery.

"Sam, he's hurt," pleaded Bobby.

"Is that what this is about, Bean? Charlie fights for his life and all you can think about is your dick?"

"Leave it, Sam," said Bobby.

"Ain't like that," said Bean quietly.

"Are you going to fuck up this band because you've got a broken heart, is that it?"

"Fucking hypocrite," Bean muttered.

Sam felt his anger explode. "What did you say?"

Bean's eyes were wet with tears. "I called you . . . a no talent leech cunt," he screamed.

Sam smacked Bean across the face.

"Call me a cunt!"

"Fuck off!" shouted Bean holding his face.

Sam lunged at Bean, grabbing him by the scruff of this neck.

"Sam! Stop it!" shouted Bobby.

Sam was already dragging Bean towards the door. He pulled him down the corridor as Bean staggered, fighting for balance. Sam pulled open the front door and hurled him out into the driveway. He fell heavily on the gravel. Rix grabbed Sam from behind.

"What the fuck are you playing at?"

As Sam struggled to break free from Rix's grasp, Bobby and Sherry joined the effort, pushing him against the wall of the hallway.

"You're a sorry excuse for a human being. You're dead weight! You hear me?" Sam shouted down at Bean.

"I wish it weren't Charlie lying in that hospital. He's worth a million of you." Bean struggled to his feet and ran across the drive.

"Get off my fucking property, cunt!" Sam called.

Rix shoved Sam back into the house and went after Bean.

"What's with you, Sam?" said Bobby. "Have you completely lost the plot?" She rushed out of the door to follow Rix. Sam made a grab for her. "Bobby, get back here!"

Bean was already out in the road when they caught him.

"Bean! Wait!" Rix caught him by the arm. Bean spun round to face them, his cheeks glistening with tears. "C'mon, let's sort this out. We're all a bit fucked up at the moment."

"He's the one who's fucked up. He wants to destroy our sound!"

"No one's going to destroy our sound," said Bobby. "He's just doing what he thinks is right."

"We don't need him, Rix," Bean pleaded. "Let's get our stuff and find someone else."

Rix pointed to Sam's garage.

"Half the stuff in there is his, Bean. Besides, where we going to go?" Rix looked around him with embarrassment. Bean could not believe what he was hearing. "Think about it.

Henry. His old man. All his life Sam's been surrounded by music." He sighed. "Look, if you can't think of him as a friend, at least think of him as a meal ticket . . ."

Bean looked across to the house. Sam stood defiantly in the doorway.

"You're a fucking sell-out too." Bean turned and began to run up the road. "Fuck you! Fuck all of you!"

9

Bean picked his pint glass off the bar and unsteadily poured the last of the lager into his mouth. The bell had already sounded for last orders.

"Jacky," he called and slapped his hand on the bar. "Service, yeah?" Bean was drunk. He'd been drinking since he got back to the estate. Drinking to forget all about Sam and Rix and Rachel. Bean knew his place now. It was right back where he had started, on the estate among the dirt and concrete and despair.

Jacky, the barman, was a red-faced Irishman. He looked at Bean slumped over his empty glass and laughed heartily.

"Jacky. Get some take-outs, yeah?" muttered Bean without looking up.

Jacky laughed again, shaking his meaty head. "We don't see you in here since you're a nipper. Then you turns ups and makes up for it all in one night. I dunno."

Bean sorted through his change on the bar. It was mainly coppers.

"Look, Bean, have this one on the house." Jacky came round to Bean's side of the bar and handed him a can. He helped Bean towards the door. "Not only do you not look like your old man, you sure as fuck can't drink like him." He opened the door and nudged Bean out into the night. "You take care, all right?"

Bean stood limply in the streetlight and toasted Jacky with his can.

"'Kin' great, Jacky! No . . . no . . . p . . . p . . . fucking thanks."

Jacky smiled and closed the door.

Bean stretched his eyes open as he tried to get the block where he lived in focus. Satisfied, he stumbled down the centre of the road. He tucked the can under his arm and pulled out a crumpled packet of cigarettes. He shoved one into the side of his mouth and patted his pockets for a box of matches.

Bean didn't hear the car until it was too late. There was the crunch of brakes on wet concrete and he was engulfed in light. He dropped his matches and threw a hand over his eyes. The car had stopped barely a foot in front of him. Behind the two bright rectangles of the car's headlights, the driver's door swung open. A solid heavy beat thundered from inside the car and a dark figure climbed out.

"ABS brakes," the driver said "You know it makes sense!"

Bean shook his head in confusion.

The driver moved around to the front of the car and picked up Bean's matches. He struck one. The light from the flame lit up the driver's face. Elroy!

"Homesick, were we?" said Elroy as he lit Bean's cigarette.

Bean's head rolled on his shoulders as he inhaled. "I ain't got no home."

Charlie watched the hypnotic row of lights flashing along the roof as he was wheeled fast down a long corridor. He was still reeling from the pain of being moved from his bed. Now, strapped into a thin cot, his mind cleared and the panic returned.

"I don't want to go," he said.

"What was that?" Charlie heard a bell ring and a lift's doors slide open. A green-suited paramedic bent down over his face as they wheeled him into the lift. "You all right, mate?"

"I don't wanna go too far . . ."

The lift doors closed.

"Cause you do, mate. Stoke Mandeville's the Rolls-Royce of spinal care. Fresh air, rolling hills, lovely . . ." As the lift climbed the paramedic chatted to his colleague.

"What about United on Saturday, then?"

"Tell me about it. Giggsy played a dream!"

"He's world class. Absolutely world class."

"Wasted on those Taffys."

"Beckham," started Charlie, "he's the best for my money."

There was a pause. The lift shuddered to a halt and the door slid open, filling it with the darkness of the night. On the roof it was a cold and windy. The sound of the helicopter's rotor blades was deafening.

"Might get a crack at Europe this year," shouted the paramedic over the din.

"Don't want to go too far," said Charlie. But no one heard him.

Elroy lived high above the city, on the twenty-fifth floor of the largest tower block on the Ferrier estate. Bean watched his own reflection in the black glass of Elroy's window. Beyond it were nothing but the grey building and orange neon of the city's lights. He felt at home looking out over the silence and the nothingness.

Elroy busied himself at small table.

"Bean, get your white ass over here."

Bean joined Elroy at the table and sat down opposite him on a ratty sofa. Elroy was filling the tin-foil bowl of a makeshift pipe.

"This one's on me," he said. "A toast to the day we slap that bloodclot Sam Jackson up real bad. Learn that rich boy some fucking manners."

Bean took a swig from his can.

Elroy handed Bean the pipe. "There. Beautiful."

Bean took the pipe without a word. Out of habit he puckered and sucked his lips before he put the mouthpiece to his lips. Elroy stuck two matches and lowered them gently to the bowl. "We gonna dark them up . . ."

Bean sucked on the pipe. A plume of white smoke filled the plastic chamber and then rushed towards him, biting at the back of his throat. He coughed blowing smoke out through his nostrils. "Don't fucking waste it. Smoke it, go wan . . ."

Bean inhaled deeply and held the smoke down.

"That's it. Keep it there, bro."

As Bean exhaled he felt a warm energy spread from his feet right up through his body. The energy seemed to gain speed and intensity until it exploded in a white flash across his eyes.

"Fuck mine!" Bean fell breathless back on the couch. The last thing he saw was Elroy smiling as he lit the pipe at his own lips.

"Yeah, man!" he laughed. "You going up . . ."

★

Charlie closed his eyes as he felt the ground fall away behind him. He couldn't see it but he knew the helicopter was carrying him up and away from everything. Strangely the noise and darkness of the little cockpit were a relief from the fear; at least he knew where he was for now. As he left London, he flew away from Lucy, from his friends and from his life. A life that was never meant to be. He closed his eyes and prayed that he would never have to go back down.

10

The monitor screen swarmed with a blurred pattern of black and grey shapes.

"That's it?" said Sherry.

"Wait a second" said the nurse as she rolled the ultrasound pad back over the bump of Sherry's glistening stomach.

"There it is!" said Bobby, bouncing on the spot with excitement. The pattern changed shape to reveal a tiny white foetus.

"Oh, my God," said Sherry. Her eyes misted up.

"Look, Rix. My baby." Sherry grabbed Rix's hand.

"Yeah." He wore a huge grin.

"Well, it looks pretty healthy to me," said the nurse.

"I don't want to know," said Sherry. "It'll be beautiful, boy or a girl."

"You don't have to know."

"I do," said Bobby. Rix and Sherry looked at her sternly. She shrugged. "So I can start shopping."

Bean turned his collar up against the cold. He leant forward to look up and down the road. Nothing but a few rusty cars and a scrubby patch of grass for dogs to shit on. All around him graffiti on brick walls and huge concrete towers growing out of the ground as far as he could see. He let the cigarette fall from his mouth and onto the concrete pavement.

He took another look. A young man about his age was walking briskly down the street towards him. With a look over each shoulder he ducked into the doorway and joined Bean. He handed him a couple of crumpled twenties. Bean took the money and nodded. He spat a ball of crack wrapped in polythene out of his mouth and passed it to him.

"Cheers, Bean."

"Later."

Bean jogged across the road and up a long walkway which

101

led into the base of Elroy's block. The acrid smell of piss led him to metal door of the lift. Bean stabbed at the button to call it. When there was no response, he swore and started for the stairs. Taking them two at a time, he headed up. By the time he reached the twenty-fifth floor he was sweating and breathless. He rounded the corner onto Elroy's balcony to see two guys standing by the open lift door aimlessly talking; one held the lift door open with his foot.

"Arseholes."

Bean reached Elroy's door. It had been modified, a flat plate of impenetrable steel welded across it. The windows on either side of the door were barred and had been boarded up from inside. Bean fished out his key, which hung on a chain around his neck, and let himself in.

Daylight did nothing to enhance the ambience of Elroy's flat. It was a tip. The sofas were covered with discarded clothes and tabloid newspapers. The tables had disappeared under a rubbish of half-converted coke bottles, beer cans and overflowing ashtrays. Elroy himself lay back in an overstuffed but threadbare lounger in front of an immense state-of-the-art TV. He was taking a hit on his pipe as Bean entered.

"Fucking hell," Bean grimaced. The flat stank like rotting fish.

Elroy exhaled grandly. "Little Billy called. Outside in ten!"

"Fuck that! I just bin down there!"

Elroy swung round. "I don't give a fuck. You've been staying in my house for a month, eating my food, paying no rent. Smoking my fucking gear. You wanna play you gotta pay!"

Bean cringed and walked through the kitchen. The scene was the same: dirty crockery and take-out boxes covered every surface. Bean pulled open the freezer. Sat on the ice was a half-finished box of mint choc chip ice creams and a re-sealable polythene bag of crack rocks.

"The usual?" he called.

There was no reply. Elroy had gone back to watching TV. Bean passed him and headed for the door.

"Cash," he growled.

"Oh, yeah." Bean put a ball of notes into Elroy's out-stretched hand.

"Don't be ripping me off, man," warned Elroy.

"Respect, man." Bean was hurt. They were meant to be friends.

There was a squeal of rubber on linoleum as a wheelchair came to a sharp halt in front of Lucy.

"Wanna lift?" said a man in a neatly creased Manchester United shirt. "Got real smooth ride . . ."

Lucy looked down at the smiling face of the wheelchair's occupant and laughed.

"Hi, Mick. Got a new shirt?"

"Latest strip . . . take it off so you can have a closer look, if you like." Mick took his hands off his wheels and peeled up his Manchester United shirt to flash his stomach.

"That's very kind of you. Maybe another time."

Lucy stepped past him and carried on through the ward, swinging a plastic supermarket bag by her side. All around her the ward hummed with frenetic daytime activity. Physio-therapists worked with arms and legs, visitors chatted and nurses flustered past with trolleys or piles of sheets. A TV played a daytime soap opera in the corner.

Lucy reached Charlie's bed and planted a kiss on his forehead.

"Hello, sweetheart," she said breezily.

Charlie had lost weight; where once he had been rake thin now he was gaunt; his thick quiff of hair had been cut short and his chin was dusted with blond stubble. Most of his machines had gone but he was left with a lightweight tin flap attached to his neck to breath through. His iron crown too had been removed; a couple of dull purple marks on his fore-head were its only legacy. Charlie though was as immobile as ever. He smiled as Lucy sat on edge of the bed so he could see her in a row of angled mirrors suspended above his head.

"Hello, sweet cheeks."

Mick appeared beside her.

"Still not working, Mick?" asked Charlie.

"Mate, it's a long life."

Lucy pushed a strand of hair off Charlie's forehead.

"He's on his last warning. Again! Gonna throw him off the ward if he don't chill out."

"I'm a bad man, Charles. If you want, Lucy, you can spank me. I need the discipline . . ."

"Don't push your luck, Mick," she replied. Lucy pulled an apple out of her bag and tossed it into Mick's lap. "Now buzz off."

Mick gave a dirty laugh and wheeled into the ward. Lucy tipped the rest of the contents of her bag into the fruit bowl by Charlie's bed.

"Hungry?"

"I dream about you," said Charlie quietly.

"Yeah?"

Charlie watched Lucy's back as she tidied his night table.

"I make love to you every night." Lucy froze. "Like everything's normal . . . and just for a moment I think . . . that when I wake up . . . it will be."

Lucy closed her eyes and prayed.

Sam was watching Iona through the thick glass of the studio's recording booth. Henry had fronted him the money for studio time. He was now installed in Henry's office with his own desk and a secretary on loan. He even had interest in the band from Buzz at Rough Line; if he could come up with the right sound, and the right sound meant a vocalist and a decent demo. Sam knew it was all he needed, a chance to get the sound ready to sell. Rix was a different matter though. Between Charlie, Bean's disappearance and Sherry's pregnancy, he'd been in no mood to discuss the band. At the end of the day Sam knew he'd come round and he had. Rix needed this more than anyone.

Sam nodded his head in time to the sweet soul of Iona's song playing through two playback speakers above him. She was talented, using lyrics she'd written the night before to Rix's music. As she sang, she read them from a thick sheaf of notes on her lap. Henry was right when he said Iona was drop-dead gorgeous. She had coffee skin and oval eyes; a cable of thick braids hung down her back. And yeah, she could really sing.

As she finished, Sam hit the switch for the studio mike.

"Wicked, Iona! Excellent!"

Rix and Bobby were not impressed with Sam's efforts. Bobby sat on a stool next to the engineer while Rix stretched across a sofa at the back of the studio pretending to read a magazine.

"Sorry, I'm a little hoarse today." Iona's voice boomed through the speakers. Bobby sniggered.

"Don't take the piss, Bob," warned Sam. He touched the switch again. "No problem, babe! Sounds great from here."

"Babe! Since when did she become babe?"

Iona cut in again.

"Middle eight needs a little work. Bass messes with the vocals."

"You're fucking joking, right?" said Rix from the shadows.

"Okay, okay. Calm down. Let's just humour her for a moment. Iona, we'll run it again."

She nodded.

"Fuck this!" said Rix. He got up to leave.

"Rix, wait. Bobby, talk some sense into him," he pleaded.

Bobby shrugged. "Why?"

"Okay, I'm ready."

"Iona, just a sec . . ." Sam blocked Rix's path.

"Get out of my way, Sam."

"Rix, come on. She's got 'fuck me' written all over her forehead. She's perfect!"

"What!" said Bobby.

Sam held up his hand to calm her protest.

Iona squinted at the booth

"Hello? You don't like my suggestions?"

Sam hit the switch again.

"No, no, no, they're great. Just getting the tape ready."

"They're great, are they?" said Rix, seething.

"We always knew she'd be difficult, yeah? We've gotta stick with it. This will pay off."

"What, when you fuck her you mean," said Bobby.

Sam sighed. "What the fuck is going on here? I'm working my arse off for you two and all I get is this shit. Jealous and precious! That'd be a great name for this fucking band!"

Rix shook his head and pushed past Sam.

"Listen, I ain't got time for politics, are we working or not?" boomed Iona.

"We're working," said Sam into the mike.

Iona pointed to Rix as he stormed out of the studio. "What's with him?"

"Nothing. You know, musicians. Take five, darling. I'll just get him . . ."

Sam followed Rix down the hall and grabbed his elbow. "Rix! Chill out. Don't blow this. We need a vocalist and you know she's perfect."

"Perfect!" said Rix with a snort. "Why? Because Henry says so. Because she's got 'fuck me' written all over her. What about Bean?"

"I called him."

"You talked to him?"

"Yeah. I promised I would and I did. What do you want me to do? He never showed, end of story."

"You're lying."

Sam stood back.

"Tell you what, Rix, why don't you get Bean to manage you? Because he ain't fucking interested. Never fucking was. And from what I hear all he gives a fuck about is his next rock. So if you don't believe me, you call him."

Rix lowered his head in defeat.

"I tried."

"Listen. After all this time, we're finally there. I thought you two would be over the moon."

Rix pointed towards the studio.

"She's got her head up her arse."

"Maybe she does, but right now we need her."

"She don't fuck with my music."

Sam put his hand on Rix's shoulder in an attempt as sincerity. "She won't, I promise. Come on."

They walked back into the studio.

"Now, will you at least think about this middle eight?" said Sam.

Rix nodded. Sam opened the door of the booth. He grinned in triumph as Rix went inside. As the door shut behind him, Bobby said, "You really don't give a shit, do you?"

"What?" Sam looked at her in disbelief.

"You know what hurts me the most? All these years I've only been a fuck to you, haven't I, Sam?"

The engineer stood and walked out without a word.

"Hey, wait!" said Sam. The engineer waved over his shoulder. Sam sighed. Bobby was still looking hard at him.

"I just wish I'd been able to fuck you back . . ."

"Oh, come on. Look around you. This is it, you've arrived, the little girl's dream. No more singing in the mirror with a fucking hairbrush."

"I never wanted this, Sam. All I ever wanted was you . . ." Sam smiled weakly. "But now that's over . . ."

"Over? C'mon, Bob . . . you don't mean that?"

Bobby walked over to Sam and gave him a gentle kiss on the cheek. "You take care, Sam." She picked up her bass and left.

Sam stood alone at the mixing desk and watched Rix and Iona argue silently on the other side of the glass.

"Fuck!" he said bitterly.

11

Lucy sat by Charlie's bed and read to him from the day's newspaper.

"This is a great one. A man who robbed a Stoke Newington newsagent of £450 worth of scratch cards was arrested last night after he returned to the scene of the crime to collect £25 in winnings."

"Silly wanker," chuckled Charlie.

"Mr Douglas Trembell of . . ." Charlie's laughter turned into a cough. "54 . . . Northfield . . . Way." Charlie struggled for air; his throat was gurgling. Lucy looked around for a nurse but there was no one in sight. Charlie was going red. Without thinking, Lucy picked the suction tube off the wall and pressed the stud which started it. She copied the routine she had seen repeated so often and delicately lifted the tin flap in Charlie's neck. She winced as she inserted the tube through a bubble of phlegm and gently into his throat. The thin whine of the vacuum cleared the blockage. Charlie inhaled deeply as air flowed to his lungs again. As she fell back into her chair, she realised that she was shaking. "I spoke to your mother," she mumbled as she wiped her hand on a tissue. "She said she would come up to visit today."

Charlie tried to smile. He spoke through his dry throat; his voice almost a whisper.

"Sorry, darling. What?"

"I love you," said Charlie.

"I love you too." Lucy gave a brave smile.

"How long have I been like this?"

"Two months nearly.

"I want to hold you. I want to be alone with you. When I get out. I want you and me to fly away . . ." Lucy kissed him on the lips. "I've got to fly away . . ."

The water in Bean's pipe bubbled as he took a long hard

drag. He sucked the smoke deep into his lungs and blew out a grey plume that swirled in front of the TV set.

"Is that my fucking gear again, you slag?" said Elroy as he pulled on a brand-new shirt. "I'm watching you, man. You're working for every fucking penny of that."

Bean shrugged.

Elroy grabbed a bin bag from the kitchen and rushed around the flat, sweeping up handfuls of rubbish. He stopped and looked at Bean. "Anyway, what the fuck are you doing here? I fucking told you I had associates coming. You was supposed to be out." Bean went to take another hit on his pipe. "C'mon. Get the fuck out!"

"All right, man," said Bean, switching off the TV. "I'm going." He looked around with a stoned gaze for his things.

"Look at you, man, you're wasted."

Bean grinned.

"Yeah, well, it's my day off."

The door bell rang.

"Fuck! You gotta hide!"

"Hide?" said Bean.

The doorbell rang again, pushed twice impatiently.

"Bollocks! Say nothing, right? Nothing!" Elroy tossed the bin bag into the kitchen and brushed down his shirt. He unbolted the door.

"Ricky! Wassup?"

Two huge West Indians wandered into the flat. The first was tall and well built with a dyed blond crew cut. He flexed his muscular body under a short leather coat, pushed Elroy to one side and moved purposefully into the room. He checked the bedrooms then walked across to the kitchen and looked inside. Satisfied, he stopped in front of Bean. He looked him up and down, grinning to expose a row of gold teeth. Then he shoved Bean hard, flinging him back onto the sofa.

Ricky stayed by the door. He wore a fine cut silk suit which strained over his thick muscular torso. An expensive raincoat was draped across his shoulders. He too stared at Bean with suspicion.

"Who'd fock is dis?" he said in a broad Jamaican accent.

His eyes narrowed with anger. The atmosphere dropped a few degrees. He didn't look like a man to be crossed.

"Me don't like surprises, Elroy. Specially the white ones."

Elroy was flustered. Bean was meant to be long gone and Ricky had a reputation for unpredictable and spectacular violence.

"He's safe, man. Known 'im since school. We're lifers." He turned to Ricky for a reaction. He seemed calm. "Listen, man . . . I'm moving a lot more. I told you I needed help."

Ricky sucked his teeth and walked over to Bean. He gestured for him to stand so that they were level.

"Never trust a white man, my mama tell me. Their history's tattooed on our skin."

Bean met Ricky's gaze through half-closed stoned eyes. He spoke to him slowly and deliberately.

"I never fucked anybody over in my life, who didn't have it coming to him, you got that? All I have in this world is my balls, and my word, and I don't break 'em for no one, you understand?"

There was a stunned silence. Elroy shook his head.

"The fucker's lost it."

"*Scarface*," said Ricky. He flashed his teeth.

"Scarface, what the fuck is that?" said Elroy.

"A motion picture, fool. See why everybody say you is totally ignorant . . ." Ricky sucked his teeth again. Then he pressed his muscled finger into Bean's chest.

"You work for Elroy. Never come to me for nuffin? Never talk business wid I. Never call my name. Me want you, me call you. You understand?" Bean nodded. Ricky turned back to Elroy. "He fuck up, me come looking for you" Elroy shifted nervously.

"Yeah, Ricky, cool." Ricky rolled his head to stretch the tension from his neck.

"Now, what me doing here?"

"Moving more than ever, Ricky," said Elroy. "I need bigger pick-ups. You know, expand my enterprise a little."

Ricky's bodyguard shoved Bean back into the sofa.

"You want it, me got it," said Ricky. "Just want a return on

111

me investment." Ricky nodded to the bodyguard, who swept back his coat to reveal the heavy black pistol tucked into his belt. He pulled a block of crack the size of a tennis ball out of the inside pocket of his jacket and tossed it to Elroy.

Elroy caught it, wide-eyed.

"Move dis for me quickly," said Ricky.

"No problem."

Ricky patted the side of Elroy's face and laughed. He turned and walked to the door.

"We gone!" he called over his shoulder.

The bodyguard was still staring at Bean. Bean stared at the gun resting at eye level, inches away from him. The bodyguard smiled as he folded his coat carefully around the gun and followed Ricky out.

Elroy dropped the crack on the table and showed them out. Bean hopped off the sofa and picked up the ball of crack. Unwrapping it, he scraped off enough for a pipe and went to work.

"I told you to keep it shut," shouted Elroy as he came back in.

"Why ain't you got a gun?" said Bean as he put a match to his pipe.

"What?"

"Gonna need a gun. You're just a fucking boy otherwise."

Elroy clipped Bean over the back of the head.

"Oi!"

He grabbed the ball out of Bean's hands and sat down opposite him. He ran his fingers over the smooth surface of the pale yellow lump.

"Look at that. Beautiful shit. I'm gonna make some real money here, man. Maybe get me a Beamer. No, a Merc. Chrome to the max."

Bean blew out his smoke and sniffed.

"Gotta get a gun," he giggled. "Got a gun, got respect."

"You're fucked, you know that?" said Elroy.

Bean put a second match to his pipe and inhaled. Elroy shook his head.

"So . . . good shit, eh?"

Bean blew out a cloud and gave him a thumbs-up.

Sam left the studio late. Things hadn't got much better after Bobby left. Rix and Iona had continued to tear lumps off each other, arguing about fifths and segues and a whole bunch of stuff which to him just seemed like wasting a lot of expensive studio time. Sam did his best to calm things down but he felt like telling both of them to fuck off and doing the record himself. Around nine the engineer announced his departure.

"That's your time up, mate," he said cheerfully and cut the power.

Rix left without a word, staring daggers at Sam. Iona was no better. Sam checked in with Henry, who laughed and told him he was learning the job the way he had. Then he hung around the office for a while smoking cigarettes. He didn't feel like going home. With no Bobby waiting and Rix barely talking to him there didn't seem a lot of point.

He let himself out around ten-thirty and wandered round to the car park. His day hit rock bottom when he saw his Truimph. All four tyres had been slashed

"Oh fuck! No fucking way," Sam shouted as he ran towards the car. Someone had even gone to the trouble of snapping off a wing mirror and using it to gouge a hole in the canvas roof. The stereo had been crudely ripped out to leave a bent metal frame and a cluster of wires. Sam sighed and sat on the bonnet. He looked around him in the darkness for help but there was no one in sight. Shaking his head, he put his hands in his pockets and walked off into the night.

Sam wandered through the empty streets, slowly falling into a daze. The click of his heels of the wet pavement like slow metronome to his thoughts.

As he cut through a side street, ahead of him he saw two people tumble out of a shuttered pub.

"Sort yourselves out!" shouted the publican as he slammed the door on them. They shouting at each other. A young man and woman arguing. The man became more and more abusive. He lunged at the woman, grabbing her by the scruff of the neck and dragging her along the road. The woman wriggled out of his grasp but he lunged at her again. Sam ran towards them and pulled the man off.

"Easy, mate. She's half your size." The man turned and spat at him visciously.

"Fuck off! Nosy fucking bastard." It was Chris, Rachel's sometime boyfriend, inflamed with rage.

"Stop it! Stop it!" Rachel was hysterical.

Chris lunged at her again. Sam swung him round and punched him hard on the side of the head. Stunned he staggered sideways. Sam kicked the back of his legs and he fell to the ground, scrabbling away across the road. He turned to Rachel. She was shaking and brushed her hair back trying to calm herself.

"You all right?" asked Sam.

She nodded and looked at him in metallic light of a streetlamp.

"You! You're Bean's friend," said Rachel, recognising Sam. "And you're . . ."

"Rachel . . . Fancy meeting you here."

Sam smiled.

"My pleasure." He gave a mock bow.

Chris came at Sam again out of the shadows. He swung a rusty metal pipe which caught him on the forehead. Sam staggered back, dazed by the blow.

"Bastard!" Rachel screamed and kicked Chris with all her might in the groin. Chris dropped the pipe and bent double.

"You idiot! That's the limit!" She grabbed hold of his hair and swung him around. Kicking him again as she did.

"Ouchhh! All right! Let go my hair!" After a final kick in the arse, he ran off.

"Just fuck off!" she shouted after him. Rachel hurried over to Sam.

"Wonder woman . . . saved my life," he said as he dabbed at his forehead.

"It's me should be thanking you . . . He's a total arsehole!" Rachel looked at the cut above his eye with some concern. "Look, you're bleeding!"

"It's nothing."

"Least let me put a plaster on that for you. I live right here."

Sam shrugged. Rachel took hold of his arm and led him over to her house.

Sam was still there as the sun rose over Canary Wharf. They had spent the night together on Rachel's roof, lounging in deck chairs. Talking for hours and eating a makeshift meal of leftovers from Rachel's fridge. They wrapped themselves in blankets for warmth against the daybreak chill and looked out over the river as the city woke up and the first lonely barges made their way out to sea.

"People always leave me . . ." said Sam as he drained his glass. He put the glass down next to an empty wine bottle.

"What do you mean?" said Rachel.

"I dunno, somehow they let me down. My dad, Charlie, Bean, now Bobby." Sam fingered the plaster on his forehead. "Let's just say, I've learnt to rely on me."

"What happened to Bean?" asked Rachel as she nibbled a biscuit. "Had a bit of a thing for him, but he never called . . ."

"Dumped me too. I mean, we had a bit of a disagreement and he just walked . . ." Sam shook his head. "Just when things starting to look up for the band. I tried to keep him from throwing it away but he wouldn't have it."

Rachel looked out over the city.

"Life's too fucking serious . . . one minute everything's easy, just having a laugh, then bang! Suddenly it's all so complicated."

They fell silent and watched as shafts of blue cut through the early morning sky.

"Dawn already." Sam stood up with a blanket still draped over his shoulders and stretched. "I talk too much, kept you up all night."

Rachel stood up to face him. "No worries, that's what the weekend's for . . ."

"It all your fault, you know . . . you're much too easy to talk to . . ." He yawned. "Time to go and face the day."

"Yeah," said Rachel. She shivered and wrapped her blanket tighter around herself.

"Yeah" said Sam. He looked at her for a while. Her face was radiant in the light of the fresh day. She seemed to smile slightly. Without a word he engulfed her in his blanket and they kissed.

12

Lucy patted the orange pap on Charlie's plate into a small pile and scooped it up with a fork. She curled her tongue over her lip in concentration as she wobbled it off the plate and spooned it into Charlie's mouth.

"I think I'm getting the hang of this."

Mick whizzed past in his chair.

"Eh up, someone's got company." Lucy caught sight of Rix, Sherry and Bobby coming down the ward. They looked like they were on their way to a picnic. The girls carried polythene bags of fruit and bunches of flowers. Rix swung his ghetto blaster by his side.

"Charlie, look who's here!" said Lucy.

Rix's grinning black face from a dozen angles loomed in the mirrors above Charlie's head.

"Hey, Charlie! What happening, bro?" Rix pinched Charlie's cheek.

"Hello, sexy," said Sherry as she and Bobby placed smacking kisses on his forehead. "Sorry we didn't call. We went flat-hunting on the weekend."

Rix winked at Sherry as she shrugged off her coat. She blushed.

"You'll have to excuse us, we're having our dinner," announced Lucy. She had scooped up another forkful and now held it in front of Charlie's mouth.

"Lucy!"

"You've got to feed your body to help it recover," said Bobby matter-of-factly.

Charlie took the spoonful.

"That wasn't so bad," said Lucy.

Bobby rubbed his leg.

"He's been a very good boy."

"Leave it out," said Rix with a frown. He reached into the pocket of his jeans and pulled out a cassette. He held it to Charlie's mirrors so that he could see the Perspex box. "You, my friend, are in for a treat." He set the ghetto blaster up on Charlie's night table. "Our very first tune. Top bollocks, studio quality. Just listen." Rix popped the tape from its box and slid it into his ghetto blaster. When the assembled crowd had settled in their seats, he pressed the play button.

The music had the same raw magic that he remembered from all those afternoons in Sam's garage but the studio had smoothed out all the edges. It poured like liquid from the speakers. Charlie beamed.

"This is fucking brilliant, Rix." He nodded his head in time to the beat.

Lucy had prepared another forkful and put it to Charlie's mouth.

"Lucy, I really don't . . ." He struggled to evade the fork.

"Doctor said if you eat well you'll be out sooner . . ."

"Yeah, mate, back on your feet," called Mick.

Charlie opened his mouth.

"See, Charlie, almost finished." Lucy scraped the last of the food into a final pile.

"Lucy, please, no more. I'm trying to listen . . ."

"You can listen to it in a minute . . . your food's getting cold."

Charlie rolled his head sharply away from the fork. "I said, I don't want any fucking more!" he shouted.

Lucy jerked with fright, dropping a dollop onto Charlie's chest. Defeated, she lowered the fork onto the plate with a click. Charlie closed his eyes tight . . . Mick understood all too well. He shook his head and wheeled gently away. It was Bobby who broke the silence. She stepped silently forward and wiped the pulp off him with her handkerchief.

"Who's for a cup of tea or something?" said Sherry.

Lucy switched off the music. "I'd better get rid of these things," she said, holding up the fork and plate.

"Yeah, come on," said Bobby. "Girly chat, eh?"

Charlie opened his eyes as the girls moved away. "Sorry," he said.

Lucy stopped. "That's okay," she said flatly.

"See you in a bit."

"See you in a bit," said Bobby.

"Sorry, mate."

"Don't even say it, mate."

"Thanks. The little bit I heard I loved. What'd you say her name was?"

"I didn't but it's Iona. I brought a couple of tapes for you and I'll leave the boom box. Ani asks if she can visit. Mum says it's okay . . ."

"Rix," Charlie interrupted. "The box, you can't. You ain't been parted from that thing since you was fifteen."

"What? It'll be safe with you. You can give it back to me when you get out of this place."

"Nice one." Charlie paused. "I see Sherry's starting to show."

Rix raised an eyebrow.

"Yeah?"

"Is that okay? I mean with you."

"It's good."

"Just good?"

Rix rubbed the back of his head with embarrassment.

"Yeah, good."

"So you really want it . . . You and Sherry?"

"Want what?" Rix played dumb.

"The kid, Rix, the kid. Pay attention!" said Charlie, grinning.

"Yeah." He smirked. "It's what we do, ain't it? What we're here for. But I dunno. Can you imagine one of us with a kid?" Charlie's smile faded. "Shit, Charlie. I'm sorry. I didn't think."

"Life don't seem so precious till you realise you don't have one," Charlie said. He closed his eyes again. "She's going to leave me."

"What?" said Rix.

"Lucy."

"No, man. Don't say that. Lucy wouldn't."

"Rix, look at me. She's twenty-two. How can I ask her to deal with this?"

"Charlie, give it a chance."

119

Charlie turned to Rix. "To see you walk out of here . . . that's hard. But to see her and not know if she'll be back. That's unbearable." Rix felt the weight of his words. "I'm tired of all this, Rix. Believe me, she is going to leave me."

"Give it time, Charlie."

Mick popped his head round Charlie's curtain.

"We've got nothing but time, mate."

Charlie sniffed. "It don't get much worse than this."

Bean and Elroy sat on a park bench in the middle of the flat empty plain of Blackheath. At their feet lay one of the roads which neatly traversed the heath, cutting it into quarters. Periodically a car rushed past them, taking a short cut through the park.

Bean looked pasty and nervous. Selling ten-quid deals in the street was one thing but this was a whole different ball game. He tugged hard on his cigarette, crushing the heat of the butt flat between his fingers. Elroy acted casual. He leant back across the bench, a beer bottle hanging loosely from one hand.

An expensive sports car cruised slowly past them. The driver looked firmly ahead, paying them no attention. It stopped fifty yards from them.

"That's our man," said Elroy quietly. "Remember, smooth. Like a fucking magician. Swap, don't talk and then we walk."

Bean looked at the car and shook his head.

"Why the fuck have I got to do it?"

Elroy leant in close to him and hissed, "I told you, Bean. You pay to play with me." Bean looked at the car again. The driver flashed his emergency lights. The signal.

"Fuck it," said Bean. Elroy nudged him hard in the ribs then slapped a brown paper package into his chest. Bean looked at Elroy and winced. He shook his head again and dropped his butt on the ground.

Bean stood up and took a long look around the heath. He could see no one; just a kite, a few kids and residential build-ings like doll's houses in the distance. He started to walk towards the car. His feet felt heavy, each step an effort despite the mechanical thumping of his heart. There was a foul taste of metal in his mouth and his head swam. As he reached the car, he caught a glimpse of his reflection in the driver's window; he looked like he was about to cry. The window slid smoothly down. Inside a white man in a shiny track suit sat on beige leather. He looked straight ahead, eyes fixed on some imaginary point in the distance.

"You're new," he said.

"Yeah."

Bean handed him the brown paper package. The man took it and dropped it casually on the passenger seat next to him.

"In the boot." The window began to slide up as the words left his mouth.

Breathless, Bean walked around to the back of the car. Its boot popped open in anticipation. Inside was a brand-new Puma sports bag. Bean lifted it out and shut the lid with his free hand. The car pulled away. The whole exchange had taken under a minute

"Fuck mine," muttered Bean as he headed back to the bench. Elroy was nodding with appreciation as he approached. But Bean felt close to collapsing, his breath echoing in his head with each unsteady step. He sat down heavily next to Elroy and put the bag at his feet.

"Nice one . . ." said Elroy. Elroy knocked back the last of his beer and dropped the bottle on the grass. He grabbed the bag from between Bean's feet. "We're out of here."

"There a fucking bin there," said Bean, pointing at a round concrete bin next to the bench.

"What?"

"Bin. There. Pick up your rubbish and put it in the fucking bin!"

Elroy burst out laughing.

"You fucking serious?"

Bean nodded.

"You brought it here . . . You drank it, so you put it in the fucking bin! This is the only clean space around. Respect it."

Elroy sucked his teeth and picked up the bottle. He dropped it in the bin.

"You're fucking mental, you know that? Come on." Elroy walked off. Bean followed. He was grinning from ear to ear as he swaggered after Elroy. He felt ten feet tall and rising.

Rix had never been to Henry's office before. When he called Sam to say that he wanted to talk about the band, he had insisted it be there. He knew Henry was loaded but, as his only experience of offices was work experience at a local insurance firm, he was not ready for the thick carpets and wood panelling of South East Management. Even the lifts were gold-plated. As the doors slid open he nervously rubbed his scuffed trainers on the back of his legs and turned down the collar of his jacket before entering. He gave his name to a pretty receptionist who pointed him down the hall.

Sam's office was small but just as luxurious as the rest of the place. At its centre was a huge dark wooden table; classy-looking paintings hung on the walls, along with a few gold discs. He knocked tentatively on the open door. Sam was marching back and forth in front of his desk, talking into a hands-free telephone. He wore a suit, a new one that Rix didn't recognise. He looked every inch the successful businessman.

"We've been over this before," he barked at the phone on his desk. He waved Rix towards an armchair. "Listen, mate, read the contract then we'll talk." Sam shook his head bitterly then shouted, "Don't fucking play games with me!" He slammed the phone down.

"What's that all about?" asked Rix.

"Pissing contest," said Sam. "In case you're wondering, I won."

"Glad you're on our side, mate."

Sam smiled.

"Seen Charlie lately?" continued Rix.

Sam's face dropped. "Yeah. Called him a couple of days ago." He sat down behind his desk and changed the subject. "Anyway. You called me. What's on your mind?"

"I . . ." Rix flushed.

122

"Everything okay with Iona? The session going okay?"

"She's a bloody pain in the arse, but I guess things are coming along."

"Just needs her ego tickled from time to time." Sam looked at his watch and swore. "I'm sorry, mate, I've got someone coming. I gotta go in a minute."

"I need to talk to you," said Rix.

"I know, mate," said Sam standing. "We'll do it later, I promise."

"Look, Sam. Sherry ain't working. We need a down payment on a flat . . . I'm in the studio all day . . . It's just that there's the kid to think of now . . ." Rix looked at his feet. "And there ain't no money coming in."

Sam paused, watching Rix's embarrassment across the table, nodded as Rix spoke. Pulling his gold Parker pen from his pocket he traced a pattern on his blotter,

"You need an advance?" Rix shrugged.

"Yeah."

Sam raised an eyebrow and smiled. He leant back in his chair and planted his feet on the table.

"So you slag me off for getting a singer. You threaten to walk out on the band just as I'm cutting a substantial deal and then you come and ask me for money."

"Fuck it! Don't know why I bother." Rix stood up to leave.

"Can't have it both ways, Rix." Sam's words stopped Rix in his tracks. Sam opened his desk drawer and pulled out a sheaf of papers. "Standard contracts. Already drawn up." He tossed the papers onto the desk in front of Rix. "It's give and take. I gotta know you're committed."

Rix stared at Sam. "How long have you had these?"

"That's not important. All I need is your signature on the first three pages and you can buy all the nappies you want." Sam pulled off the cap of his pen and offered it to Rix. "You should have come to me straight away," said Sam. "I'd have lent you the money from my own pocket."

Rix shook his head grimly.

"I'd rather have the money from the deal if it's all the same to you." He signed the first sheet.

"Suit yourself."

There was a knock on the door. Rix spun round to see Rachel standing on the threshold. She held a big sunflower.

"I'm not interrupting anything, am I?"

Rix looked at Sam.

"Course not, baby, we're just finishing."

Rix signed the final two pages and dropped Sam's pen like it was dog shit onto the pile of papers.

"You're Rix, right?" said Rachel.

Rix said nothing.

"I'll have a cheque for you tomorrow morning, yeah?" said Sam.

"Come on, sweetheart, we've got a table."

Sam took Rachel's arm. Rix watched them walk out. As they went he wondered what the papers that he'd just signed were going to cost him.

13

Dr Carmichael was the ward specialist. He was a wiry and nervous man with wild, unkempt hair that gave him the air of a mad scientist. He pulled the pleated green curtain around Charlie's bed for privacy and then greeted Mr and Mrs Rowntree briskly. Lucy offered to make him a cup of tea, which he declined. He pulled up a chair next to Charlie's bed.

"Right, Charlie," he said as he flipped over the top sheet on his clipboard. "From your X-rays, my colleagues and I have determined the swelling in your vertebrae has finally receded." He rested the clipboard on his lap. "Your physio tells me that you have some sensation below your chest which is encouraging, but there's little improvement in your mobility . . ."

"Will I walk again?" said Charlie bluntly.

Lucy placed a reassuring hand on his arm.

"It's doubtful."

Charlie's mother caught her breath.

"My hands?"

Dr Carmichael shook his head. "I'm afraid they too will experience minimal movement . . . I'm sorry."

Lucy put her hand to her mouth in shock.

"Oh, sweetheart," said his mother, clinging tighter to her husband's hand.

"Quadriplegic. Isn't that what they call it? Fuck." Charlie rolled his head away from the doctor.

"Charlie, you must remember this is an initial diagnosis. Things may still improve."

"Fuck!" shouted Charlie. "Oh fuck, oh fuck!"

"Charlie, don't . . ." said Mrs Rowntree, her eyes overflowing with tears. Charlie too was crying, sniffing back great waves of emotion.

"Fuck!" As he looked at the concerned faces of his family reflected above him, he steadied himself, shaking his head to clear his eyes. "I'll be okay," he said.

"Charlie," continued Dr Carmichael, "Stoke Mandeville has . . ."

"Leave me alone. I wanna be alone."

"Very well." The doctor turned to Charlie's parents. "Could I show you to the family room?"

"We really should be going. Miss the traffic and all."

"We really should discuss planning for Charlie's long-term care."

Charlie's dad nodded. "Yes, of course." He helped his wife to her feet.

"I'll see you later, love." His mum kissed Charlie's wet cheeks.

"We'll beat this, son," said Charlie's dad, his voice cracking as he spoke. "We won't let it get on top of us."

Charlie remained silent. He stared at the ceiling.

Lucy busied herself picking up the bags and newspaper Charlie's parents had brought with them. She thanked the doctor and kissed Mrs Rowntree before they disappeared through a flap in the curtain.

When they had gone, Lucy turned back to Charlie. After all that had happened, he seemed calm. He was stretching his tongue right out, curling it over to dab at the end of his own nose. Lucy smiled.

"What's all this about?"

"Touching the end of my nose." Charlie dabbed again. "Sam could pick his . . ."

Lucy laughed. "From small acorns do great oaks grow." She kissed Charlie on the forehead. As she pulled back she saw his face had turned dark and deadly serious.

"Take off your clothes," he whispered.

"What? Now."

"The curtains are closed."

"What if someone comes in?"

"They won't." Lucy shifted with embarrassment. "Go on."

She unbuttoned her blouse and pulled its tails free from her jeans. "This is crazy," she said.

Charlie watched her moving in his mirror. The curves and smooth skin of her body revealed themselves from under

126

cotton and denim, resonating with the images of her that tormented his dreams. When Lucy's warmth seemed so far out of reach.

"My . . . face . . ." he whispered from behind closed eyes.

"Charlie," she said quietly.

"Please . . ."

Lucy padded across to Charlie's bed and climbed on. Lying next to him, she touched his cheek, pulling his face towards her. She kissed him on the mouth for the first time since the accident. Charlie turned away.

"My face," he demanded. Lucy moved to position herself above him. She lowered herself towards his face. She closed her eyes as his mouth touched her, a strange forgotten sensation. As he worked she moved her hips. Tears swelled in her eyes and rolled down her cheeks as she gripped the bed head trying to draw strength from the love she once knew. But it was no good.

"I can't." She dropped off him.

Charlie looked up at her tear-streaked face, mortified.

"I'm sorry, Charlie." Sniffing back the tears, she folded her arms across her chest.

"I wish I had come in you that day," said Charlie.

Lucy turned her back on him and hurriedly dressed.

Bean was bent over double coughing when Elroy came in. He sat on the sofa as usual, the TV blaring in front of him.

"Christ, man!" said Elroy.

Bean looked up and smiled to reveal raw gums. His pallid skin was flushed from his exertions. He sniffed a ball of phlegm back down his throat and swallowed.

"Aperitif!" He wiped the tears out of his eyes with the collar of his jacket and went back to stuffing his pipe. He put the mouthpiece to his cracked, sore-covered lips and lit up. When he had finished he lay back into the sofa and closed his eyes. His lips moved slowly as they tried to suck some moisture back into his dry mouth.

He was oblivious to Elroy as he reached into his jacket and pulled out a heavy black automatic pistol. The first he knew

127

of it was the touch of cold hard metal against his temple. He stared up to see an ugly-looking gun barrel moving in front of his eyes. Elroy's grinning face was behind it.

"Fucking hell!"

Elroy laughed and spun the weapon in his hand like a gunfighter.

"Pretty scary, looking down the barrel of an automatic flesh-ripping piece of hard cunt, eh?"

Bean looked confused. "Where the fuck did you get that?"

"Tools of the trade, mate," said Elroy. Elroy swung the gun at the end of his outstretched arm around the room, squinting along the top of the sight. "Any hassle and . . ." Elroy targeted an empty beer bottle which lay in one corner. "Bang." The gun leapt in Elroy's hand, spitting a six-inch tongue of flame. There was a sickening metallic crack and a blinding flash as it discharged in Elroy's living room. "Shit!" Elroy staggered backwards, staring at the smoking gun in disbelief. The bullet had smashed the bottle into pieces and had chipped a hole in the wall. "Loaded . . . It's fucking loaded."

Bean rubbed his ears and laughed. "Fink I've gone deaf." He leapt up from the sofa in total awe of the gun and grabbed it from Elroy. He took his turn striking poses around the room. He stopped in front of a cracked mirror and pointed the gun at his reflection. "You looking at me? I said . . . You looking at me?"

Elroy was still stunned by the gunshot. He sat down on the sofa and massaged the tingle of the gun's recoil out of his hand.

"He never said it was fucking loaded."

"Hey!" said Bean as he pressed the barrel of his gun to the side of his face. "Bean McCormack. Licensed to kill." He chuckled.

Elroy shook his head in disbelief. "Licensed to be a cunt more like."

Most nights, in the dark of the ward, Mick would park his wheelchair next to Charlie's bed and they'd talk. The nights were long in the ward. He and Charlie would lie awake together, trying to fight the demons of solitude, though some nights, as Charlie cried on the other side of the curtain, Mick knew it was best to leave him alone. For the most part, Mick's optimism and dirty humour helped keep Charlie's mind from torturous dreams of Lucy. The nurses warned them to keep it down but Mick was a hard character to stay angry at for long.

"So it turns out this 'she' was a 'he' all along," said Mick in a stage whisper.

"You are fucking kidding me!"

"Would I joke about something like that?"

"Jesus. So what happened?"

"Well, my mate figures he's paid good money, right? So why waste it."

"He didn't?" Charlie laughed in disbelief.

"He fucking did. He flips her over and . . ."

"Do you mind! Some of us are trying to sleep," shouted an angry voice from the other side of the ward.

"No, we don't mind," called Mick as he and Charlie collapsed in hysterics.

"The dirty fucking bastard . . ."

Lucy parked in the empty car park of the hospital. She switched off the ignition and sat in the dark. She hated the late visits. The terrible darkness and despair of the ward and Charlie's tears in the harsh electric light. She felt so very tired. Across the way was a square of yellow light: the French windows which led to Charlie's ward. She could see shadows moving in the light. Nurses dishing out cocoa and turning down beds. As she watched the movement of the window she thought back over the events of that evening. Lucy had stayed late to avoid the traffic on the way out to Stoke Mandeville. She had been caught crying in the ladies' loos by Jeffrey, one of the firm's partners. He was locking up, not expecting anyone to be left in the office. He had been so kind. Even asked if she fancied a drink. It had been a long time since she had been treated as a woman rather than a nurse.

Drawing on the last of her courage, she picked up a bag of

fruit and a magazine from the passenger seat and got out of the car.

"You see me coming?" said Mick. Charlie nodded with his eyes still closed. "I'm making a run for it. Giggs and Beckham on my arse . . . Posh Spice is there in the crowd screaming. David, Davie boy, man on!" Charlie giggled at Mick's falsetto.

"Yeah, I see you."

"Boom! Off my right foot, ball arcs away, higher and higher . . ."

"The crowd roars . . ." continued Charlie. " . . .drowning out Giggs's screams of frustration! Out of nowhere Rowntree, number eleven, emerges unmarked."

Lucy stopped halfway down the ward. Ahead of her she saw Charlie and Mick illuminated by Charlie's night light. Mick was hunched conspiratorially next to Charlie's head. She heard them talking, running free in their minds with the memories of bodies no longer theirs.

"He's coming after the ball, but he's got a lot of ground to cover if he's to be on the receiving end of this one . . ."

"Come on, Rowntree, come on." Mick mimicked the gravely sound of the cheering crowd.

"Got my eye on it . . . No one else exists, just me and the ball. As it falls back to earth, I'm there to meet it . . . Oh no, just out of reach!"

Lucy felt the warm swell of tears but nothing came; she was done crying. As she heard Charlie talk in her mind she saw him in the park on those sunny afternoons after school. Charlie's flashing smile and fancy football flicks. The Charlie who chased her, the Charlie who climbed to the roof of the world without fear. He was gone. She put the bag of fruit down on a table and turned to go.

"He leaps! Soars! Airborne. Nearly horizontal!" shouted Mick.

"Will you be quiet!" called the angry voice.

"I strike! It connects! A guided missile straight for the back of the net."

"Crowd goes silent," said Mick. "Jaws drop. Beckham falls to his knees. A religious moment . . . then . . ."

Together they screamed: "Goooooooaaaaaaaal!"

By the time Lucy reached the end of the ward she had made up her mind. She would never return.

Elroy's flat was a million miles away, misty under a thin haze of crack smoke. Elroy was slouched across the sofa. On his knee sat a giggling sixteen-year-old girl in a pleated school skirt. Her mother, Sharon, sat next to them, sucking hard on a pipe. As she blew out smoke she looked around Elroy's gloomy flat. Even with the lights low you could see that it was a tip. The bottles, cigarette butts and take-out cartons they had got through during the night were illuminated by the blue glow of the big TV.

"Not exactly the fucking Ritz, this place," said Sharon.

Elroy kneaded the young girl's breast.

"Stop it," she said with a giggle.

"Your daughter's got nice titties."

Sharon laughed as she re-lit the pipe. "Well, you know where they came from, lover."

"Let's have a look then." Elroy pulled down her top to reveal her breasts hanging in a dirty bra.

"Fuck off!"

Elroy gave a dirty laugh.

The noise of a muffled trumpet scale came through the wall from Bean's room. The music was weak; notes were missing and the final flurry was a weak sigh of his former brilliance. Elroy jumped.

"What the fuck is that?"

"Trumpet, I think," replied Sharon flatly.

Elroy sat up sharply and the girl slid off his lap. She grabbed at the pipe hungrily.

Elroy strode across to the wall and thumped on it.

"Shut the fuck up, man, I'm trying to chill." The trumpet went silent. "Fucking hell!"

When Elroy returned to the sofa, the girl was already blowing out smoke. She put the pipe down and slid her arms around Elroy's neck. A grinning Elroy slid his hand up her skirt.

"I thought it sounded quite good," said Sharon.

"Why don't you fuck off now, Mum." The girl giggled. "I'm in safe hands."

"Charming," said Sharon. She got up and reached for one of the balls of crack on the table. "I'll just entertain myself."

Elroy slapped her hand. "Fuck off, you greedy slag!" he said. "Go see Bean." Sharon shrugged. "And tell him to stick his horn!"

Sharon went over to Bean's door and let herself in.

"How are we Bean, love?" she said as she entered.

Bean stood in the centre of the room looking out blankly across London. His trumpet hung loosely by his side. In his other was a still-smoking pipe.

"You've got a visitor," she sang, trying to get through to him. Sharon moved around in front of him, smiling into his glassy eyes. "Don't you worry about Elroy. He just got a bit of a temper." Sharon eyed Bean's pipe. "Tell you what? Why don't I do something for you and you can do something for me?"

Bean narrowed his eyes to focus on her.

Sharon knelt in front of Bean and began to undo his trousers. Bean looked beyond his reflection and out into nothingness.

14

Sam cut the office early and drove over to the studio to check how Rix and Iona were getting on. He parked his, now repaired, car and headed straight for the booth.

"How we doing?" he asked the engineer, patting him lightly on the back. The engineer looked at Sam and shook his head wearily. "That good, huh?"

"You've picked a right pair."

In the studio Iona was trying to sing her lyrics over soft piano notes picked out by Rix on an electronic keyboard. She threw her notes down in frustration as the music missed her lyrics time and time again. Sam let himself into the studio. He picked up a chair and flipped it round before straddling it.

"New? I ain't heard this. Could be the single we're looking for."

Rix stopped playing on a bum note. Iona clucked her tongue and shook her head. Neither of them looked pleased to see him.

"No, it ain't, and you ain't likely to again either. It's crap," said Rix.

"It wouldn't be so crap if you knew how to play," replied Iona.

"Hey," said Sam, trying to diffuse the atmosphere. "Look, we're all tired; how about we break and get back to it tomorrow?"

"It ain't going to make any difference, Sam," said Rix.

"That's positive." Iona dropped her lyrics into her bag.

"Listen, guys, if this ain't working why not try playing something else?"

Rix was angry. "Like what, Sam. You got anything up your sleeve?"

"Come on, Rix. You know what I mean."

"Do I?" said Rix sarcastically. "How about this?" Rix touched a button on his synth. The room was filled with the sound of Bean's trumpet. One of his swirling climbing scales.

133

"Very funny."

The beat kicked, smooth as chocolate. Iona jumped up, her eyes wide with excitement. Sam looked startled. He spoke gruffly to Rix in his businessman voice. "This is bit busy for Iona. Better without."

"Leave it!" said Iona.

Rix nodded with a grin.

Iona began to dance to the music as if possessed with cool rhythm. As Bean's melodies told their story she sang her lyrics over the top, complementing Bean's subtle notes with her own. It was perfect.

"That's enough" said Sam. He leant across Rix and switched off the music.

Iona pulled off her headphones and looked across at Rix.

"That was wicked, Rix!" She held out her hands in excitement. "Look at me, I'm shaking . . ."

Rix swivelled on his chair to face Sam.

"Sam reckons it's a bit too busy for you."

"What the fuck does he know?" said Iona. "He's only a manager."

Rix beamed with new-found respect. "Yeah."

"Anyway, we can't use it," said Sam, fuming. "Legal reasons."

"Oh yes we can," said Iona. "And we're going to." Rix was blushing at her enthusiasm. "I can't believe you held out on me. What is this song?"

"It's called Bean's Song."

Sam got up and went back into the booth.

"Bean?"

"Yeah? He's an old mate of mine." He smiled. "We used to be partners."

"You know where he is now?"

"Yeah, sort of . . ."

"Well, let's get him in!"

It took Rix most of the night to find Bean. Everyone he called seemed to think his old friend had vanished off the face of the earth. His own feelings of guilt kept him awake, as did

Sherry, who tossed and turned in the bed next to him, trying to find some way to get comfortable with the weight of her belly. Around six a.m. he ended up wandering round the Ferrier estate. He gave a fiver to some guy from his old school, Thomas Tallis, shivering in a doorway. The guy looked like he didn't know what day it was. He eyes were glazed and, despite the cold, he was sweating. But he knew where Elroy lived all right; it turned out that he and Bean were largely responsible for his condition.

As the sun came up, Rix stood outside the solid steel door of Elroy's flat. Figuring they'd be used to visitors at all hours, he hammered on the metal with his fist. Eventually he heard sounds of movement behind the door. Bolts clicked back and Bean peered out.

Bean wore a ragged dressing gown; there was a heavy gold chain around his neck and when he smiled at Rix there was gold in his teeth.

"Wow, Rix, man," he croaked sleepily. "Cool. How the fuck you been?" said Bean without enthusiasm.

He ushered him into the flat. Rix was knocked back by the smell. The place was covered in rubbish. Elroy and a girl lay comatose on the sofa. Bean beckoned him into the kitchen and flicked on the harsh striplight.

"Long time, bro." Bean sat down at the kitchen table and went through various discarded cigarette packets until he found a smoke. "What can I get you?" he said, lighting up.

"Nothing, thanks." Rix sat down and looked around at the dirty kitchen in disgust.

"How you been, man?"

"Trying to get on with it."

"Ain't we all?" said Bean.

"Bean, we got a deal, good money. One of the tracks is yours, man." Rix pulled a cassette from his pocket and placed it on the table. Bean lounged in his chair, brooding. Eventually he spoke in Elroy phoney-Jamaican patois: "Don't need that shit no more. We make twice in a week what you slags earn in a year, you get me? Take my tunes as a birthday present, Rix." He cackled. "Sorry, I ain't got no card or nuthin."

Rix heard movement behind him. He saw Sharon shuffle out of Bean's room wrapped in a filthy towel. She muttered something and then went into the bathroom.

"Bean, we gotta get you out of this place."

Bean stared at him then snorted. "Yeah, bwoy! Listen, why don't you chill a while. Have a spliff, get to know a few of your brethren here . . ."

"My what?" said Rix, appalled.

"You know what I mean . . . your people and that." Bean swept his hand majestically across the filthy flat.

"My people? These ain't my people. They got nothing to do with me. You was my people, Bean. We was best mates, for fuck's sake." Bean's face hardened. He shook his head. There was a pipe on the table. He pulled a ball of crack and a lighter from his pocket and began to fill it.

"Don't give me no fucking lecture."

"How could you dump us like that?"

Bean put the pipe to his lips. "Fuck you talking about?"

"Sam called you and you blew us out."

Bean blew out smoke. "Never did."

"Bollocks, you just pissed your mind away on that pipe."

Bean lunged across the table and grabbed Rix by the throat. "Shut it! He never called. Never!"

Rix fell back, his eyes wide, stunned by Bean's new-found violence. "What?"

Bean let him go with a coy smile. "It don't matter, eh? I got what I want. I'm where I wanna be. That's my people asleep out there and this is my home. Always was, you see, that's where I went wrong . . ." Bean struck his lighter again. "Hanging out with you cunts . . ."

Rix watched him as he sucked down another caustic lung full. "You remember a cunt called Charlie? Yeah?"

Bean's eyes narrowed with fury.

"Get the fuck out of my house." Bean leapt up and grabbed Rix by the collar, jerking him out of his seat. "Don't fucking need you. I don't need nothing." He shoved Rix through the flat. He opened the front door and swung him roughly out onto the landing. Before Rix could turn to face him, Bean had slammed shut the door behind him.

Rix brushed down his coat. He looked at the cold steel of the reinforced door in disbelief. Finally, he stuffed his hands in his pocket and headed home.

Inside the flat, Rix's sudden departure had roused Elroy.

"Bean, man," he whined, still half asleep. "If you're going to fuck that bitch do it quietly, yeah."

Bean went back to the kitchen. He dropped into his chair and reached for his pipe. The cassette that Rix had brought was still sitting on the table. He picked it up and turned it over in his hand. "Bean's Song" had been written on the box in felt tip.

Mick watched Dr Carmichael as he walked down the ward. He was pushing a brand-new wheelchair in front of him. Two nurses had already spent the best part of the last hour setting up a portable winch next to Charlie's bed. Charlie had stared impassively at the roof as they had rolled him from side to side to slide a sling underneath his wasted body and fit a temporary neck support. He had not asked them what they were doing because he already knew. As the doctor approached, Mick bit his lip with concern. He knew what it was like to spend your first day in a chair, what it was like to know for the first time the unbearable pain of your body's failure.

Dr Carmichael parked the wheelchair at the end of the bed and flicked on the brake with his foot.

"Right! Are we all set?" he said breezily.

The nurse nodded.

"All right, Charlie," she said. "I'm going to need you to help me with this."

"I'm not sure that I'm quite ready for this," said Charlie.

"Of course you are. It's time you got out of this bed and mobile."

The physio switched on the winch. Its electric motor whirred and the sling tightened round Charlie's body, slowly lifting him off the bed. Charlie gave a scream of pain.

"Come on, Charlie," said the nurse. "You've got to work with me."

Charlie gritted his teeth in agony as six months of immobility was stretched out of his body.

"I can't do this." Charlie shut his eyes and tried to ride the pain as the blood surged back into his numb flesh. He was lifted up a few inches above the counterpane and swung gently over his bed. "Please, I can't," he hissed. The motor stopped, leaving Charlie suspended in the sling as if he had collapsed into a deep beanbag.

"Okay. Let's move him to the chair," said Dr Carmichael.

Mick watched as Charlie opened his eyes and saw the wheel- chair for the first time. Charlie was taking it all in fast; the foot plates for his limp, useless feet; its extended rests for his lolling arms; the flat black seat in which he would spend the rest of his life. As Charlie glared at this construction of steel bars and leather webbing, Mick could see the nausea rise in him; the terrible panic sweeping across his face; his eyes damp with despair as he faced his prison on wheels. Mick was not surprised when Charlie started screaming.

"Come on, Charlie," urged the nurse.

"I can't. I can't," shouted Charlie.

Mick could take it no more.

"What are you doing to him? Fucking stop it!"

"All right, Mick, calm down," said a nurse.

"Calm down! What the fuck are you doing to him?"

"Just one last hike, Charlie," said Dr Carmichael.

Mick swung himself around to a stop between Charlie and the wheelchair.

"I said, leave him the fuck alone! He got his whole fucking life to do this."

Dr Carmichael was startled. He looked at Charlie, whose face and neck were contorted and strained with panic. Tears cut across his red cheeks.

"All right. Nurse, let's get him back on the bed. That was a good effort, Charlie. We'll try again tomorrow."

As they lowered Charlie back onto his bed, Mick stayed by

his side. Charlie was covered with sweat; he panted for breath above the neck brace.

"You all right, mate?" asked Mick as he wiped Charlie's brow with the corner of his counterpane.

Charlie nodded. "Thanks, mate."

"Any time. Got to look out for each other, eh?"

The nurse unhooked the sling and pulled the winch away from Charlie's bed. Dr Carmichael made a note on Charlie's chart and then wandered off along the corridor, leaving the wheelchair where it stood.

"I don't know what happened. The chair, I . . ."

Mick dabbed his head again.

"Forget about it. Hey, fancy a game of football?"

15

"South East Management," said Sam to the bouncer. "We're here to see the band." Rachel stood meekly behind him, slightly embarrassed at pushing in in front of such a long queue. The bouncer checked a long printed list.

"Okay," he said as his ticked Sam's name off. A second bouncer unhooked a purple braid rope to let them past. Rachel giggled.

"This is the life."

"Don't want to waste time with the riff-raff," said Sam. He was about to enter the club when he saw Lucy in the crowd. Sam walked over to her.

"Lucy, all right?"

Lucy flushed with shock. "Sam!"

"How you been?"

"Oh, you know, okay. You?"

"Great! What are you doing here?"

"We're here to see the band," said a well-dressed man beside her.

Sam looked at him, then back to Lucy. She smiled with embarrassment. "This is Jeffrey. We work together."

Sam and Jeffrey shook hands.

"All right, Jeffrey. You remember Rachel, right?" Rachel gave a little wave from behind Sam.

"You going in or not?" said the bouncer.

"Yeah. Listen, how about we grab a drink inside?"

Lucy slid her arm around Jeffrey's. "Thanks, but actually we were just going to eat. Weren't we?"

Jeffrey looked surprised. "Yes. We only came on the off chance. Bit bored queuing."

"See you around, yeah?" said Sam.

Lucy and Jeffrey disappeared into the crowd. Sam put an arm around Rachel to usher her in.

"Well, what do you know," he said.

★

The little club was packed. A reggae band played on stage, illuminated with multicoloured stage lights. The well-dressed clubbing crowd thronged around the dance floor, talking and drinking imported beer. Every few seconds a laser cut across the top of the assembled heads and wrote the name of the club night's sponsor on the wall above the bar.

Rachel went to check in her coat and Sam pushed his way to the bar to join the assembly of A&R knocking back their complimentary beers. He leant back on the hard wood and looked around the club. This was what he'd wanted all his life, not just the club and not just Rachel; he wanted the business, just like his dad, and that afternoon when an Island executive signed the band's contract he'd got it.

Through the gloom he saw Rix sitting alone in a booth nursing a glass of Scotch. Sam turned to the barman.

"You got champagne?" The barman nodded. "Make it cold, eh?" Sam bought a bottle with a fifty, then he and Rachel pushed their way through the throng to Rix's table.

"Rix!" said Sam, plonking the bottle down in front of him. "I got news, *good* news." He slid into the booth. "Island signed the contract this afternoon! We've fucking done it, mate."

"Nice," said Rix flatly.

"Nice!" Sam's smile faded. "Nice? What the fuck's that?"

Rix looked across his drink at Sam.

"You seen Bean lately?"

"What?" said Sam.

"Because I've seen him."

Rachel looked puzzled.

"Sam?"

"Rix, I don't need this right now."

"Oh, yeah? What do you fucking need? You obviously don't need to get laid!"

"Shut your fucking mouth, Rix."

"Doing all right in that department, are you? Or should you be thanking Bean?"

"You ungrateful cunt!"

Rachel stood up.

142

"This is turning into a private party . . ."

Rix grabbed her wrist. "He was in love with you, you know." He cocked his thumb at Sam. "Now this fucker's got his music and his woman . . ."

"I'm not anyone's woman, Rix," said Rachel.

Sam cut in. "He wasn't fucking interested, mate."

"Liar!" Rix spat. "You never even fucking called him! You sold him out. And for what? The latest trainers, the newest sunglasses. You swim about in this shit like a gold-medallist, *mate!*"

"This is bollocks!" Sam stood up. "Come on, Rachel."

She shook her head. "Not till I find out what's going on here."

"Know what breaks my heart?" continued Rix. "You used Charlie to kick Bean out of your house . . . out of our lives, but you never once visited him in hospital!"

Sam grabbed Rix by the collar and pulled him to his feet. "Fuck you! He's like a brother to me."

Rix glared at him, and the fire in Sam's eyes subsided and he let go. Rix brushed himself down. "Glad I ain't your brother." Rix shouldered past Sam and disappeared into the crowd.

Sam watched him go. When he turned back to Rachel, she too was looking at him with disgust.

"What?" said Sam. "What are you looking at?"

"You lied to me about Bean."

Sam sighed. "Rachel," he pleaded, "He was a total loser."

Rachel couldn't believe what she was hearing. "I'm going home."

"Rachel!"

"You still worried about everyone leaving you, Sam?" she asked. "Well, I would be, because it's just happened again." She turned and followed Rix out into the crowd.

On the other side of London, Bean lay alone on his bed, staring into nothing. He was still angry with Rix. How he'd sold out their music to please Sam and how he'd come here trying to make it right with shit about music and money.

143

Music was never about money for Bean. Music was beauty and freedom. Rix was no different from Sam.

He thought about another pipe to block out. Use his lungs to escape as he'd always done. As he scanned the room for his gear, his eyes caught a flash of gold. He sat up and pulled a filthy T-shirt off the chair at the end of his bed. His trumpet lay under it. He couldn't remember when he last played it, but it still shone. Probably the only clean thing left in the flat.

Bean reached into the pocket of his dressing gown and pulled out the tape Rix had brought. It all seemed so far away. Even Rix had come and gone like a ghost. He dropped the cassette into a tape recorder by his bed and pressed play.

There was a hiss as the tape rolled then he heard his trumpet; his beautiful sound. Leaning back on the bed, he shut his eyes and let the music warm him from inside. The sound of his horn carried him up and away from the Ferrier. As the beat came in, Bean was immersed; he floated above it all. Every familiar note was like a sweet flash of pleasure. He was walking through an orchard of music heavy with fruit. Then Iona's voice, like an angel. He thought of Rachel and how she had made him feel so complete. It was the purest thing he'd ever heard. Bean lay there and let everything else melt away. Right then he knew there was somewhere else for him and he wanted to go there.

16

Charlie's hands slipped from the rungs of his wheels. He was sweating heavily, his body completely unused to exercise. He wore gloves to protect his hands and improve his grip but his disability meant that his fingers were bent tight across his palms in a rictal claw. The gloves made little difference. He took a deep breath and tried again, propelling himself another couple of feet down the hall.

With a squeal of rubber Mick appeared beside him.

"Christ!" said Charlie, holding his hand to his chest in horror. "You scared the life out of me."

"Mick, slow down!" said a nurse as she walked past.

"I don't see no speed limit," he said with a wink and made a grab for the nurse's bum. "Last day, mate."

"I'll miss you."

"Yeah . . . time to leave the old nest."

"I don't think they could handle you for much longer. They'd have to put down speed bumps."

"Hey! Can't go on defending my crown for ever . . . Race you to the lift and back! Come on . . . Let's see what you're made of . . ."

Charlie grabbed his wheels. "You got no chance."

"Prove it," said Mick. He brought his chair in line with Charlie's. "They're under starter's orders and . . . they're off!" Mick whizzed ahead as Charlie wobbled forwards, veering crazily from one side of the corridor to the other. "The victor and all-time reigning champion!" shouted Mick with his arms in the air.

Charlie finally wheeled up to Mick, exhausted. His wheelchair bumped into Mick's with a clack.

"Christ! I'm knackered," Charlie wheezed.

"You're going to have to do better than that, boyo."

Charlie shook his head, trying to catch his breath. "One day."

"We've had a laugh, haven't we?" said Mick.

"Yeah."

"I'm trying to imagine what a romantic moment might be like when I get out. You know. Pull a bird, get her home. Like a drink? Yes . . . Music? Barry Manilow . . . Sorry, haven't got any. What about some Oasis? . . . The evening progresses. I wheel closer for a kiss . . . passion builds. My face nuzzles between her incredibly large breasts."

"I know, and then she slips a disc trying to lift you into bed."

They crack up.

"Where you going anyhow?"

"Me own place. A nice little council flat. That'll do me." Mick looked suddenly sad. "You going to visit me?"

"Sure I will. That's if you think you'll miss us."

"I'll miss those," said Mick as he pointed at a busty physiotherapist.

She gave a weary smile. "Mick! Final check-up."

Mick wheeled towards her. "How about a final bed bath, just for old time's sake?"

Bean swore and took another drag on his cigarette. Autumn had come to the Ferrier; not that there were any trees to lose their leaves, but it was bitterly cold. As he'd finished for the day he didn't see why he should wait for Elroy if he was going to end up with hypothermia. He hunched closer to the concrete pillar that supported the tower block. In the cold the Ferrier looked worse than ususal. Even the shop signs were washed out to dirty grey; there was nothing to add the slightest warmth to the view. He pulled his sports watch out of his baggy trousers. Elroy was half an hour late.

A car horn sounded urgently. Looking round the pillar, Bean saw a souped-up white Mercedes with blacked-out windows. He didn't recognise the car, not until he saw the number plate read EL R0Y.

"Fuck mine!"

The door of the car swung open to a fanfare thumping ragga. Elroy stepped out and posed next to the car. Despite the seasonal gloom he wore his sunglasses.

"What's up, Bean!"

"Where'd you get this?" Bean walked towards the car.

"Built by Germans, re-designed by the black man . . ."

"Serious piece of machinery." Bean slapped five with Elroy.

"Ain't she beautiful? Ruff and ready. A ladykiller."

Bean ran a finger along the smooth lines of the bonnet then looked up sharply. "How'd you pay for this?"

"Exchanged my old one and put a *liccle* bit of cash on top, yeah?" Elroy sat back in the car. He opened the passenger door for Bean. "A little Christmas present to myself," he said as Bean jumped in.

"Christmas ain't for weeks," Bean said, admiring the complex stereo. "Still must've cost you at least twenty G, man."

"Business is good . . ." said Elroy with a smile.

Bean frowned. "It ain't that good."

"You worry too much." Elroy grinned and floored the accelerator.

17

Elroy finished counting the huge stack of cash from a biscuit tin he normally hid behind his fridge. He sniffed it and smiled.

"There you go, Ricky, man. Fifty grand. *Beautiful*."

Ricky nodded as Elroy slid the money across his kitchen table towards his bodyguard, Blondie. Blondie put a hand on it and, sitting, began to count it again.

"What you been feeding that white boy?" said Ricky. "He's selling three times what you were."

"Yeah, but he smokes it, too," said Elroy defensively. "He's got himself a serious habit, man. We got to watch him."

Ricky let his cold eyes fall on Elroy.

"Just as long as I get me money."

Blondie tapped the stack of cash on the table to attract attention. He folded the wad and stuffed it into his coat pocket.

"Well?" said Ricky.

Blondie shook his head.

"What's up?" said Elroy, seeing the exchange.

Blondie's chair scraped sharply on the kitchen floor as he stood. He moved deliberately towards Elroy, catching him in a headlock before he could dodge out of the way. He hauled him cleanly out of his seat

"Fuck! Ricky, please," he croaked.

Blondie squeezed Elroy's neck until sweat beads burst on his bloated face. Ricky leered towards him as he gasped for breath.

"Blondie 'ere got 'O' level maths at school," he said coldly. "What you get?"

Elroy was panicking. His eyes bulged as Blondie's second squeeze forced the breath out of him.

"Answer the man."

"I didn't take no exams," he blurted.

"See that's what I tell Blondie. 'Cos he told me for two weeks now, you come up short. So either you can't count or Blondie was lying. Which one is it, fucker?"

"I was gonna tell you, Ricky, I swear. It was Bean. Bean came up short. Told me he's waiting on a debt."

"Bean. Bean! All me hear is Bean," shouted Ricky.

"He's lost it. I told you he's got himself a serious habit."

"He got a habit, you pay!" Ricky slammed his fist on the table. "That white boy is your problem." Ricky pointed an accusing finger at Elroy. "Lifers, remember?"

Blondie flicked back his coat with his free hand and pulled the pistol from his belt. He pressed its muzzle hard against Elroy's swollen temple.

"Christ, Ricky!"

"No money. Pom, pom. Understand?"

"Ricky, please. It's Bean. I can't control him. He's going around saying he works for you, using your name, under-cutting me. He'll sell to anyone, he don't care."

"Enough," Ricky said to Blondie.

Blondie dropped Elroy onto the table. Elroy coughed and massaged his neck.

"Fucking hell!"

Ricky sucked his teeth and looked around the dingy kitchen.

"One week and I'll be back. Me want all me money. Bean or no Bean."

Unable to speak Elroy lifted a hand in agreement.

Rix was balanced precariously on the side of the sofa as he leant across to put a glittery star on the top of a huge Christmas tree. "Come on! You're going to miss it."

Bobby came running in from the next room.

"This flat is brilliant. I want one."

"Finished poking around, have you? Don't know why we bothered with a surveyor." Rix wobbled. "Look, is someone going to take this picture or not?"

"Sorry." Bobby picked up a Polaroid camera that lay on the floor. "Sherry, are you gonna be in this or what?" Sherry was sprawled on the sofa. She wrestled with a bottle of champagne, which sat on top of her huge belly.

"Do I look like I'm going anywhere?" The Polaroid flashed and spat the photo.

"Thank you," said Rix, jumping down. He took the champagne from Sherry and, with great effort, opened it with a pop. He struggled to get the bottle over their glasses as the fizzy liquid spewed from its neck.

"A toast," said Bobby, grabbing a glass. "To your brilliant new place."

"To our *expensive* new place," corrected Rix.

"All right, to your expensive new place."

"Our expensive new place!"

They clinked glasses.

"Don't know how we're going to pay for it," said Sherry.

"What do you mean?" asked Bobby.

"Rix wants to leave the band."

"You're joking, right?"

Rix looked sombre.

"Don't do this, Rix," said Bobby. "I was there for all the wrong reasons but not you. It's always been your music. You are the band."

"I used to think it was Bean's music, too."

"He's just being moody, don't listen to him," said Sherry.

Rix downed his drink. He tried to change the subject. "You gonna tell us about this new 'friend' you got?"

Bobby flushed.

"No. I wanna make sure it's right, you know, before you meet."

"Bobby!" said Sherry, wriggling with excitement. She nudged her with a stockinged foot.

"Come on, who is it?"

"I'm not saying!" said Bobby, shoving her foot away playfully. "It's someone very special. Even talked me into going back to college."

"Well, that's worth a toast," said Rix.

"Wait a minute," said Bobby. She reached into her bag. "Christmas present. But open it now before I go." She tossed the package to Sherry. Sherry tore open the wrapping paper. Inside were two pairs of baby booties, one blue, one pink.

"Bobby!"

"I couldn't wait any longer. So I got you both. If it's a boy, the blue one. If it's a girl the pink."

Sherry misted up.

"Oh, Bob, they're so sweet."

"Yeah, and we can keep the spare for the next one." Rix grinned and poured another round.

"You told Charlie about this flat? I'm sure he'd be chuffed."

"I don't think Charlie's in the mood to talk about flats," said Rix coldly.

"What do you mean?"

"Heard about Mick?"

Bobby shook her head.

"Rix," Sherry warned.

"Threw himself off the top of a car park first week out. Couldn't take it."

"Oh, my God, that's awful!" said Bobby.

Sherry nodded and put the booties down. "Poor Charlie."

"Yeah," said Rix. "Poor Charlie."

Charlie looked out of the french windows at the winter gloom. Illuminated by the light from the ward, tiny flecks of snow danced in the night wind. He was so deep in thought that he didn't see Rix sit down next to him.

"All right, mate?" said Rix quietly.

Charlie nodded. Rix looked around the ward. The nurses had decorated it for Christmas. Charlie's bed had strings of tinsel taped to its metal bedpost. A selection of cards stood on his night table.

Charlie looked over to Mick's bed. He had laid a football shirt Mick had given him across the pillow.

"His Man. United disability pass came through this week. Would've had the best seats in the house."

"I'm really sorry, Charlie . . ."

"Don't be. He always saw the funny side." Charlie looked down at his twisted arms. "We never really talked about all this. Didn't have to. We was both in it together. Now I'm alone."

"Mick was alone . . . you're not."

Charlie held Rix's eye.

"He was 50 per cent better than me, Rix. He had his hands." Charlie went back to the window. "What chance do I have? If I'd just been left with my hands I could have blown my fucking brains out!"

"We'll sort it out, Charlie."

Charlie put his hand on Rix's arm. His eyes were urgent. "You're my mate, Rix. My best mate. When it comes to it, it's got to be you."

Rix sat back, reeling from what Charlie had said.

"Don't ask me to do that, Charlie."

"I'm not asking you, I'm begging."

Rix's eyes filled with tears. He shook his head in disbelief. "I won't do it. I said, we'll sort it out."

"Sort it out!" Charlie shouted. "I can't even wipe my own fucking arse!"

Rix felt himself explode. The months of frustration surged up from inside him. All the horror of being powerless to stop his best friends withering away; dying before his eyes. He wanted to drag Bean out of that dump on the Ferrier; he wanted to hug Sam so hard he would squeeze the soul back into him, the spirit of the mates he knew. But most of all he wanted Charlie to live again, he wanted to smash his ugly chair to pieces, drag him to his feet. He wanted them both to run into the night and away from this terrible place.

Rix stood up suddenly and dragged Charlie's wheelchair away from the window. He reached down to grab Charlie's legs and hauled his friend over his shoulder and out of the chair in a fireman's lift.

"Rix! What the fuck are you doing!"

Staggering under Charlie's weight, Rix leant against the door of the french windows. He turned the key in the lock and barged them open.

"You ain't fucking giving up on me," he grunted.

The duty nurse looked up from her newspaper to see what the commotion was.

"Where are you boys going?" she called. But Rix had

already lurched through the door and into the car park. "You can't go out there!"

Rix jogged across the car park, puffing with exertion, great clouds of his breath freezing in the chill air. When he reached the soft grass of its edge he collapsed with exhaustion onto one knee, rolling Charlie out onto the grass next to him.

"What the hell are you doing?" shouted the nurse, running after them.

"Please," panted Rix, holding up a placating hand. "Give us a second."

The nurse looked down at Charlie. He stared up into the moonlight, his eyes alive once more. He took a deep breath of fresh air.

"Five minutes," she said. "I don't want either of you freezing to death."

"Thanks," Rix said with a smile.

The nurse shook her head sternly and headed back inside.

Rix flopped back on the cold ground, his head next to Charlie's. Charlie was looking up into the dark blanket of the sky; it swarmed with tiny translucent snowflakes. When he'd watched the flakes in the ward, he felt so detached. He never dreamed of feeling their sharp touch and of following their intricate patterns in the air.

Charlie stuck out his tongue to catch one. A dot of ice, a sharp fresh sensation, melting on his warm flesh. It brought sensation back into his entire body. The night air moved in his lungs, making them burn with natural energy. He began to giggle. A high, uncontrollable schoolgirl giggle. Not because his senses were overloaded but because he felt his life force flood back into him.

"What?" said Rix, still struggling for breath.

Charlie laughed harder, wriggling on the ground, and soon Rix was laughing too. They laughed together and whooped up at the stars.

Charlie rolled his head over so his temple touched Rix's.

"Thanks, mate," he said.

"Happy Christmas, mate."

18

"Turn the TV on, let's have Trafalgar Square!" shouted Henry above the noise of the party. His offices were packed with New Year revellers. Henry loved Christmas so the place was decked out like a cheesy Santa's grotto. The walls were barely visible under the weight of tinsel, ribbons and crêpe paper bells. A huge Christmas tree dominated one corner of the room. "Come on, it's nearly time for the countdown." Henry waddled drunkenly over to a cupboard. Adjusting his paper party hat, he pulled open the polished wooden doors to reveal a flat-screen television set. He scanned its smooth, button-less surface for a few seconds before throwing up his arms in exasperation. "Where the fuck's the remote control? I can't turn the bastard on."

Sam sat in a big armchair swigging morosely from a bottle of champagne. Since his dad had died Christmas had not meant much to him. A selection of toiletries from his mum left subtly on the kitchen table before she left to celebrate with her boyfriend. What's more, since most of his friends were either in hospital or weren't talking to him it didn't look like New Year was going to be up to much, either.

Sam climbed out of his chair to help Henry. Henry gave a cry of pleasure and wrapped an arm around his godson's neck.

"How's our new star, eh?"

Sam smiled weakly.

"First Christmas on the firm." Henry slapped his cheek. "One of many, my darling. Just like your old man."

Sam pulled down a hidden panel on the TV and switched it on.

"Aha!" cooed Henry. "The boy's an electronic genius!" An aerial shot of Trafalgar Square packed with revellers filled the screen. Henry released Sam and turned to address the party. "Right, my beautiful guests," Henry shouted, holding up his hand to hush everyone. "Let's have that music off for the countdown!"

A cheer rippled around the office. Bodies scrummed around the set.

"Ten . . . Nine . . . Eight . . ."

Sam had had enough. He had an overwhelming desire to be with his people and maybe mend a few bridges. Ducking through the crowd, he took a final swig on the bottle. He lifted a bunch of beers from an ice box by the door and left. As the lift doors slid shut, Henry was leading the crowd in a slurred rendition of *Auld Lang Syne*.

"Three . . . two . . . one . . ." A roar went up across Trafalgar Square. "And our very best wishes for the year to come from everyone here at the BBC," said the gravel-voiced commentator. The crowd rippled and pulsated as its members hugged and danced with drunken delight. Charlie nudged the remote with his elbow and the TV screen at the foot of his bed went blank. Silence returned once again to the ward. He relaxed further back into his pillows and waited for sleep.

Sam rapped on a shiny blue door. There was a pause and then he tried again, stinging his knuckles in the cold night air. A light appeared in the glass above the door and he heard the sound of locks moving. Bobby opened it up, bleary-eyed, drunk and dressed only in an oversized T-shirt. She was still laughing as she peered out.

"Yes, hello . . ."

Sam gave her his most charming smile.

"Happy New Year, Bob." He held up the bulging bag of beers he had lifted from Henry's party. "Fancy a beer for the sake of *Auld Lang Syne*?" Bobby rubbed her eyes and blinked. A woman's voice echoed from inside the house.

"Bobby . . . I'm waiting."

"What are you doing here, Sam?" Bobby looked stern.

Sam shrugged. A young woman about Bobby's age appeared behind her. She was also in pyjamas. She slung an arm over Bobby's shoulder and kissed her tenderly on the neck.

"Who's this?" she asked, looking at the wide-eyed Sam.

156

"No one," said Bobby. "Look, I'll be up in a minute."

"Oh, sure . . .Don't be long." The woman disappeared.

Sam furrowed his brow in shock. "I didn't know," he stammered.

"How could you know anything, Sam," Bobby said flatly. "All you see is yourself. Now, what do you want?"

"I wanted to see my old mate . . ."

Bobby looked Sam up and down. "We was never mates, Sam. Look, I'm a little busy right now."

"Yeah," said Sam, stepping back. "Maybe another time, right?"

Bobby looked at Sam with sadness in her eyes. "Goodbye, Sam." She slowly closed the door.

On the doorstep, Sam took a deep breath and tried to chalk whatever he'd just seen up to experience. He checked his watch and ran a hand through his hair.

Maybe there was still time.

Rix and Sherry were woken by the sound of the phone ringing. They turned uneasily in bed as its harsh chirping rang around the flat. Rix groaned and slid his head underneath his pillow. The phone kept ringing.

"Rix . . ." Sherry moaned. "The phone." Rix mumbled. The phone rang on. Sherry poked him hard in the back with her knee. "Rix!"

"Okay, okay." Rix rolled out of bed and wandered naked through to the sitting room. He picked up the phone. "No one here," he said bluntly and dropped the receiver back into place. He switched on the answering machine and headed back to the bedroom.

Sherry had already gone back to sleep when he returned. She lay on her back with one arm thrown protectively across her eyes. The space where Rix had thrown back the covers revealed half of her huge round tummy barely covered by her nightie. Illuminated by the streetlamps outside the window the tight skin shone with a warm glow. Rix smiled as he watched the mound move up and down with her breathing. He leant across the bed and kissed his baby through the soft skin of Sherry's stomach. He slipped back under the duvet and wrapped himself around her. Within minutes he was asleep again.

Sam stayed on the line for a few seconds after Rix had hung up. He hoped somehow that his old friend had been joking. He wasn't and eventually the line went dead with a click.

Sam hung up the receiver and, picking up the bag of beer, stepped out of the phone box and into the street. He could hear laughter. At the other end of the street were a man and woman. They tumbled into a doorway, locked in a passionate embrace. He thought of the night he'd first met Rachel. With her gone he felt alone in a way he never had when Bobby left. It was as if a piece of himself had been lost. It didn't take a genius to work out what was missing from Sam's life. He had wanted Rachel since that first morning when she had slept in the hammock in his garden.

Opening the door of the Triumph, he threw the beer into the passenger seat before climbing in himself. With his hands resting on the steering wheel, he watched the couple as they giggled and groped under the stars..

"Happy New Year," he said to himself. He turned the key in the ignition and drove off into the night.

It had begun to rain by the time he reached Rachel's house. The streets shone with water. Sam huddled in a doorway opposite Rachel's front door, the street in which they had first got talking. He leant back against the door to try to stay dry. He had turned up the collar of his jacket and held it tight at the throat to keep out the winter cold. His bag of beers still hung from his right hand untouched.

A car pulled up, throbbing with music and packed with people. It parked outside the house. Rachel hopped out first. She laughed and ushered out the drunken huddle of friends who had crammed into the back seat. As they chatted on the pavement and unloaded booze and party supplies from the boot of the car, Sam hurried across the road. Rachel saw him as he moved towards her from the shadows. Her smile faded.

158

"Here, Steve." She handed her house keys to the young man next to her.

"Everything all right?" he said.

Rachel looked at the drenched Sam. "Yeah. I'll be up in a minute." Steve unlocked the door and let the group in. Rachel looked over her shoulder, waiting for her friends to disappear inside. Then she said, "I don't want to see you, Sam."

Sam's self-effacing grin crumbled. He was speechless. "But it's New Year's . . ."

"I know." She walked through her open front door.

Sam grabbed her arm. "I'm in love with you, Rachel, I need you."

Rachel tugged her arm free of Sam's grip. "I can't love a liar, Sam . . . Or a coward." She closed the door on him with a soft click.

Sam sat down on the doorstep. The street was deathly quiet again for a few seconds until upstairs he heard thumping as the first record of the night began. Sam was in shock. He had nothing and no one. Nowhere to go and nothing to do. Despite feeling the damp seep into the seat of his trousers, he reached into his bag and pulled out a beer. He pulled back the tab and took a deep swallow.

Charlie awoke with a start. An involuntary spasm rippled up his arm and across his shoulders; a final goodbye from his nervous system. His arm shivered as if electrified and flopped limply off the side of his bed. In the darkness a hand reached out and gently took hold of his wrist. It lifted Charlie's arm and laid it back across his chest. The hand of the second person covered Charlie's and stayed there.

"Fuck!" said Charlie. His eyes snapped open. He clicked on his bedside lamp with his elbow. There was a figure slumped in a chair next to his bed, silhouetted against the dawn. "Who's that?"

Sam leaned forward into the pool of light cast by Charlie's lamp.

"S'me, Charlie . . ." Sam's voice was slurred. The beer cans he had brought now stood empty at his feet.

Charlie hit the button which raised his bed. He blinked into the morning gloom, still sleepy and unsure of what he'd seen. "Sam?" he asked calmly.

Sam nodded, an exaggerated nod.

"You scared the shit out of me. How long you been here?"

"Couple of hours . . ."

"You looked fucked . . ."

Sam smiled a limp, drunken smile and brushed down his shirt front. "Am fucked . . ."

"Can I have my hand back?"

"Oh yeah, sorry . . . You cut your hair . . ."

Charlie checked his crew cut in one of his mirrors. "Got in the way, can't brush it anyway."

Sam's brow furrowed with worry. "What other things . . ." he stumbled over the words. "I mean . . ."

"Can't I do? I'm quadriplegic, Sam, got paralysis of all four limbs. Basically, fuck all . . ."

Sam looked towards the french windows. He spoke quietly: "I'm so fucking sorry, Charlie, I couldn't, I couldn't . . ." Tears filled his eyes. "I saw you, all fucked up, like my dad. Plumbed into . . . all that shit. I wanted to run, mate. Run as far away as I could. Pretend that everything was going to be all right. But it ain't going to be all right, is it, Charlie?" Sam sniffed. "It ain't gonna get better, is it? Never does." He wiped his face on the arm of his jacket and took a deep breath. "I miss my dad, mate . . . want him back. Want you to get up right now. Get up and tell me it's all right, Sam. Everything's all right now."

"I've been trying not to accept this every minute of every fucking day, mate. I've been places you don't even want to know about. The fucking fear of my life I've felt. If I could've run away, I would have smashed the world record."

"I fucked everything up. I mean, Bean, Bobby, Rix, you. I've been . . ."

"A spoilt, selfish bastard?" Charlie interrupted.

"Yeah," said Sam. He took a final swig.

"We all got our shit, Sam. You either deal with it or it'll eat you up." Charlie craned his neck to look out the window.

Dawn was breaking. "Time to deal with it . . . Help me out of bed. I wanna see what the New Year looks like."

Sam looked around nervously. "Me?" he said, pointing to his chest. "Better get the nurse, eh?"

"Sam. You'll be fine. I'll show you how. Pull the sheet back."

Sam threw back the sheet. He jumped when his saw Charlie's atrophied legs. After months of immobility they were pale and stick thin; their bones poked out as swollen white lumps under the skin.

"Like two Twiglets," said Charlie.

"Yeah."

"That's what all the girls say. Now grab my legs and pull me to the edge of the bed."

Sam took Charlie's legs gingerly and gave them a gentle tug. Charlie hardly moved. He shook his head. "I won't break. I like it rough."

"Sorry, sorry . . ." Sam heaved his friend to the edge of the bed. "Okay, got you."

"Bring the chair closer and then put my knees between yours."

Sam swivelled the chair with one hand and patted Charlie's knees into place with the other.

"Okay, now pull me up and bend me forward . . . This is the good bit . . . You get to grab my arse and I get to sniff your crotch . . ."

Sam pulled Charlie forward and flopped his arms and torso across his shoulders. "Ain't sure about this . . ." said Sam.

Charlie spoke firmly: "After three . . . all together, now! One, two, three!"

Sam hauled Charlie up. It was easier than he'd thought; Charlie was a lot lighter than he used to be. Sam turned on the spot and lowered him into his wheelchair. Sam sat back on Charlie's bed, breathing hard, but Charlie was all smiles.

"Weird, innit?"

"Mate," panted Sam. "You have no idea."

19

Bean was sitting on the loo when he heard the door of the flat slam. After nearly eight months of living together, he knew Elroy's routine backwards; they were like an old married couple. He would be swanning around the flat making out he was a big man, poking through the mess before eventually having a go at him about it.

"Fuck it." Bean turned the page of his newspaper and carried on reading. He heard Elroy clump through to the kitchen to fetch a black bin bag.

Elroy was muttering to himself as he tipped the congealed contents of ashtrays and dinner plates into it. It didn't last long. "Taking the piss!" he yelled. There was a metallic ring as an empty beer can bounced off the toilet door. "Bean!" Elroy shouted. "Are you fucking in there?"

"I'm having a shit," said Bean through the bathroom door. The bin bag was dropped outside the door.

"You're a fucking disgrace."

Bean pulled up his trousers and opened the door in front of him. "What the fuck's your problem?" he said.

Elroy's brow furrowed with anger. He pointed with menace at Bean. "You, Bean," he said bitterly. "The flat's a fucking mess and I'm working my arse off to cover your debt."

"What you talking about?"

"Your fucking debts. You pay to play, remember?" Elroy moved in close to Bean, towering over him. "Or maybe you just got sticky fingers."

Bean was outraged. "I never took nothing."

Elroy sucked his teeth. "You and that old bitch been smoking all our profits."

"What?"

"That's what happens when you're into fucking grannies, eh?"

Bean held Elroy's gaze. The triumph in Elroy's eyes made

him sick. "Actually," Bean said as he brushed some lint from Elroy's shirt front, "I've been fucking her daughter. You know, your girlfriend Stacy? She loved it."

Elroy's nostrils flared. "Don't you fucking push me."

"Lovely tight little butt hole . . . like new pussy," Bean continued. "You know what she said? She said it was the first time she'd been fucked by a real man."

Elroy shoved Bean hard in the chest, sending him flying back through the bathroom door. Elroy stepped over the bin bag and followed him through. Bean recoiled off the wall, and head first he drove all his weight to his forehead, smashing down into Elroy's face. There was a dull crack. Elroy staggered back into the living room, holding his smashed nose.

"Fucking bitch!" Blood dribbled down over his top lip and oozed through his fingers. "My fucking nose!"

Bean kicked him in the thigh and Elroy rolled back onto the sofa. Bean then snatched an empty beer bottle off the table and smashed it against the wall. Elroy looked up to see Bean standing over him, his face flushed with rage, holding the jagged stump of broken glass in one hand.

"Who's the fucking daddy?" he snarled.

"What?" said Elroy, his eyes wide with horror

"Make three times what you do. Who's the fucking daddy?"

"You are, man, you are!" Elroy held up his good arm defensively.

Bean glared down at him. "All right?" Satisfied, Bean tossed the broken bottle neck onto the table. He grinned.

"Thought we was mates," said Elroy.

"We are." Bean turned back to the bathroom, undoing his belt as he went. "What's the matter? Can't take a fucking joke?"

Elroy mopped his nose with a discarded napkin. "Yeah, can't you see me laughing?"

20

The glass doors slid open, Charlie felt his heart flutter. Rix wheeled him out into the great expanse of the hospital car park.

"Hang on a sec," said Charlie.

Rix stopped, giving him time to take it all in. Charlie looked around and blinked against the light reflected from the vast concrete square. It was dotted with cars belonging to staff and visitors. He spotted the familiar yellow of Rix's crappy transit parked fifty yards away and smiled. The van had continued to rust delightfully in his absence. It was strangely reassuring. Beyond the concrete were trees and grass, the sound of birds singing and all the things that Charlie had lost during his time in hospital. The sky looked so huge that he shuddered; it made him feel pretty small sat in the chair.

"You take care, Charlie," said a nurse. She leaned over to kiss him on the cheek.

"Thanks for everything, Louise. Don't know what I would've done without you." Louise put her arm on Charlie's shoulder and gave it a rub.

"You're a brave boy, Charlie. Make a success of things for me, eh?"

The nurse offered a cardboard box containing Charlie's possessions to Sherry.

"I'm not sure you should be carrying this in your condition." Sherry ran a hand over her giant tummy with a smile.

"Hey!" said Charlie, patting his lap. "What's this for?"

Rix squinted against the sun as he saw a familiar blue Triumph swing into the car park. He shaded his eyes with his palm and saw Sam, looking dapper in sunglasses and a business suit, was at the wheel

"I don't believe this," said Sherry.

"What the fuck's he doing here?" Rix whispered.

"Rix," warned Charlie.

Sam parked up and came bounding over. Rix glowered at him.

"Bit fucking late, ain't it?" he said.

"Wanted to be here for my mate!" Sam feigned innocence.

Rix snorted. "What?"

Charlie spoke up. "Please, both of you, don't make this any more difficult than it already is."

"I'll be in the van," said Sherry. She waddled ahead.

"Sorry," said Rix.

"'Sno problem." Sam looked over at Rix's van and chuckled. "Still travelling in style, I see. Want a hand?"

Rix nodded.

They wheeled Charlie over to Rix's van. Rix took the padlock off the back doors and fixed them open. After a count of three they lifted Charlie into the back and secured his chair in place with a web of elastic bungee cords.

"Made to measure," said Charlie. "Could be a bit cleaner, though."

"Don't you start."

Sam clapped his hands together.

"Right, meet you back at the house," he said.

Rix looked at him in disgust. "Whatever." As he climbed in through the driver's door, Sherry gave a squeak and grabbed her tummy. "What is it?" asked Rix. Sherry clasped her stomach and winced with pain. "Sherry?" Rix slid across the seat and put his arm round her. "You all right?"

She nodded. "It's nothing. I'm fine, honestly."

"Sure?"

"Yeah." She looked at Rix and smiled.

"Just as well," said Charlie from the back. "Don't think I could stand another day in hospital."

With a cough and plume of black exhaust smoke the van started.

Charlie waved one last time to Louise. As they drove along the drive, he watched her slowly fade away against the grey brick façade of the hospital. Charlie had thought about this moment a million times, turning it over in his head relentlessly in all the lonely, sleepless hours he had spent on the ward. Finally he'd faced the truth. It was time to look forward.

As they hit the motorway, Charlie leant back in his chair and relaxed in the cramped confines of the van. He watched the real world go by. A world overflowing with the movement and the energy he had captured on film The world that he'd been denied by the halo-traction, and neck collars and stretchers. He thought about Mick and wondered if there was ever to be any more place for him in this world than there'd been for his friend.

"You all right?" asked Sherry, leaning over the back of her seat.

Charlie snapped out of his daze. "Yeah. Yeah. Fine. Hey. In that box there's a tape."

Sherry rummaged in Charlie's box. "This one?" She pulled out a cassette.

"Yeah, put it on."

Rix glanced at the tape. "Don't wanna hear it, Charlie."

"I don't care, I do." Sherry slid the cassette into the battered stereo embedded in the dashboard.

The sound of G.M.T. filled the van. Iona's voice, Bean's trumpet, Rix's beats. Charlie nodded in time to the music. Rix kept his eyes fixed firmly on the road, his face clouding with anger.

"Turn it up," said Charlie. "This bit's wicked."

Sherry laughed. "You're the boss." She cranked the music up.

"I love this tune," said Charlie.

Rix slapped the palm of his hand on the wheel. "That's enough!" He stabbed at the stereo and ejected the tape. "It ain't going to work, Charlie."

Charlie looked at Sherry. She shook her head.

"I must have listened to that tape a hundred times . . ."

Rix stamped on the brakes and swerved violently towards the hard shoulder. He brought the van to a sudden halt with a crunch of gravel. He killed the engine and swung round to face Charlie.

166

"Charlie, I can't stand being around him. He's a user, a fucking manipulative little shit. I don't need it."

"Whatever you think about Sam, he did get one thing right . . . your music."

Rix clenched his fist on the back of the seat. "I ain't listening. You don't know the half of it."

Charlie held up his hands; they were bent across his wrists like shepherds' crooks.

"This must have shown you something, Rix. You've been given a chance. Don't piss it all away."

Rix gave a sarcastic grin.

"Nice try . . ." He turned the key in the ignition. " . . . but I ain't the one doing the pissing."

Charlie's parents were waiting on the doorstep of their Victorian terraced house as Rix's van pulled up. They were chatting to Sam, who had again donned an expensive pair of sunglasses against the afternoon sun. Through the thin tin walls of the van Charlie heard his mother clucking with excitement.

"Here we go," he said quietly.

"Just play it cool, mate," said Rix as he climbed out.

"Took your time," said Sam.

"Yeah, well, we had to stop." Rix unlocked the van doors.

"Welcome home, darling," said Charlie's mum. With an unusual athleticism she jumped up into the van and gave him a kiss.

"Mum!"

"Hello, Charlie," said his father from behind her. He wore an uneasy smile, made more of bravery than affection.

Sam and Rix struggled with the bungee cords holding Charlie's chair. They hauled him and his chair from the back of the van and lowered him on to the ground.

"Thank God you're home, love," said his mum as she kissed him again.

Charlie smiled weakly.

"I'll drive, shall I?" suggested Sam. He took hold of the handles of Charlie's chair and wheeled him towards the house.

Charlie looked his family's terrace up and down as he trundled towards it. It hadn't changed. He felt his guts turn. It had taken him most of his life to get out of there and now he was back. He bumped over the pavement and past the little brick wall at the foot of the front garden. He'd spent hours on that wall as a kid, dodging cars as a group of them kicked a ball around in the street.

"Wait till you see inside. Your dad's been really busy."

Sam pushed the chair over the doorstep. There was a scrape and Charlie jerked forward in his seat. He was stuck in the threshold.

"Got any Vaseline?" said Sam.

"I'm sure I measured that," said Charlie's dad.

"Take the wheels off," said Charlie flatly.

Sam and Charlie's dad held the chair as Rix popped off the wheels. They carried him down the hall and into the living room.

"Blimey!" said Charlie's dad, red-faced from exertion. "I'm going to have to get used to this."

They planted Charlie in the centre of the living room. Then they backed away as Charlie looked around in disbelief. The living room had been completely converted.

"Hope you like it, darling. Dad decorated it for you. Put some of your favourite photos up."

Charlie was open-mouthed with horror. A big hospital bed had replaced the dinning-room table. One wall was stocked with medical equipment and boxes of drugs. A shower chair from Stoke Mandeville stood in one corner. An old embroidered screen from the attic was next to it for privacy. His dad pushed open the double door which led to the garden.

"Look, son," he said pointing. "I built a ramp out into the garden. Got a good deal on the concrete from your uncle Peter."

Family photos and his mum's oil paintings had been taken down. In their place, Charlie's own photographs had been loaded into clip frames and hung in their place. Some of his sports trophies sat on the sideboard next to a TV and a large plastic piss jug. Charlie couldn't believe his eyes; his own house looked like hospital. Customised with reminders of his former life, it was a vision of hell, every inch of the room was a shrine to what he had once been.

"Good to have you home, darling." His mum stroked his hair.

Rix and Sam hung back near the doorway, taking it all in. It didn't seem right. It was a cripple's room not their mate's.

"Can I get anyone tea?" said Charlie's mum.

Rix shook his head.

"No thanks, Mrs Rowntree. I'd better be going."

"Yeah," said Sam. He patted Charlie's shoulder. "I'll call you later, maybe go out . . ."

"I'll show you out, lads," said Charlie's dad.

Charlie looked grimly at the bed. Just like back in the hospital. At the head was a picture of him as a kid playing football, poised high in the air and about to kick. He looked down at his wasted legs and felt the weight of the disability bear down on him. He grabbed his wheels and pushed himself towards the french windows. His mum instinctively went to help him.

"Here, darling, let me . . ."

"It's all right, Mum . . . I can . . ." But she was already moving him across the carpet. Charlie bit his tongue as he felt his independence slip away.

Sherry was waiting in the van as Rix emerged. He was walking fast in a effort to get away from Sam.

"Wait up, Rix," said Sam.

"I ain't interested, Sam."

"I just wanna talk about Charlie, please."

"I know you, Sam, you're just feeding your guilt trip."

Sam stopped dead in the middle of the street. He waited for Rix to take him seriously

"He can't stay like that Rix. I mean . . ."

Rix spun round and pointed at the house. "He's been like that for months!" he snarled. "And he's gonna be like that for the rest of his fucking life."

Sherry leaned across the bench seat of the van and wound down the window.

169

"Rix, please."

"Sure, he'll get money, maybe he'll even be a million-aire . . . but he's always gonna be in pain . . ."

Sam backed off, holding up his hands defensively. "I'm just saying we've gotta do something."

Sherry sucked in a breath sharply. She sat up and clasped her hands to her stomach trying to absorb the shooting pain of her first contraction.

"Rix!"

"I'm glad you fucking noticed," Rix said to Sam.

Sherry was breathing heavily, panting rhythmically and fast as she'd been taught at her antenatal class. "Oh, my God, it's starting . . ."

"What?" said Rix.

Sherry bent double in the van, her arms folded underneath her. "The fucking baby, Rix!" she shouted.

Rix froze in shock.

Sherry looked across at him with pleading eyes as pain shot across her abdomen.

"What the fuck do I do," he asked.

Sam grabbed the keys out of his hand. "Get in, I'll drive."

Charlie craned his head to hear Rix's van pull away with a rattle. He wondered briefly what the shouting was about. When the noise died down he turned back to the french windows. Down at the end of his parents' narrow garden, his dad was already pottering about in his shed. He ducked in and out of the bushes around it, poking at the earth and tweaking his plants. The end of the garden was always the best place to hide from his mum; some things never changed.

"Auntie Carol sends you her love. She's going to pop round tomorrow." Mrs Rowntree blustered in, holding a dishcloth. Charlie nodded absently, barely hearing her. "Dinner won't be for a while yet. Would you like a sandwich?"

"I'm fine, thanks."

She fluffed up the pillows on his bed then looked at her son, lingering in the room for as long as she could. Charlie felt her gaze and turned to look back at her. She pretended to

170

straighten some pictures on the wall to cover her embarrassment. She paused a while and then said, "Let me help you out
of that jumper. You must be boiling. . ." She rolled Charlie
back from the window and lifted up one of his arms to free his
pullover.

"Please, Mum." Charlie shifted uneasily in his seat as she
pulled the jumper over his head. His voice was smothered by
the thick wool. "Mum, please just leave it!"

21

Sherry's screams segued into the stuttering first cries of her child. There had been a desperate drive. Sam at the wheel, grinding the gears. Rix in the back trying to remember the breathing exercises, and Sherry flat on her back on the dusty steel floor, swearing like a trooper and driving her nails into Rix's flesh where she grabbed him.

In the delivery room, when the time came, tears had involuntarily sprung from Rix's eyes. The two sounds blended together in the warm air of the hospital, a perfect mix; he couldn't have done better if he'd had his decks.

The baby flew up from between Sherry's legs, carried by gloved hands. It seemed like only minutes since Sam had poured them through the door to the waiting whirlwind of nurses and fast-moving wheelchairs that had ended here. So suddenly there she was, wriggling into life, laid out on Sherry's tummy. Small, blue and perfect.

"I love you, baby," said Rix. He kissed Sherry on her damp forehead. He was rigid with fear and excitement and his hand throbbed from Sherry's grip. She had nearly crushed it. During the final throws of her labour Sherry was laughing and crying together as she touched her child for the first time; her hands shook with exhaustion.

"My baby."

"She's perfect," said Rix. "Just perfect." He felt a tap on his shoulder.

"Would you like to cut the umbilical cord?" said the midwife from behind her face mask.

Rix looked down at the knotty purple cord still attached to his child's navel. "What?"

"The umbilical cord?" The doctor proffered a pair of surgical scissors.

Rix wiped his eyes clear with the corner of his gown and took the scissors. Looking at Sherry, he laughed in disbelief. "Fuck mine."

★

Charlie was tired and his eyes stung from the dozens of cigarettes he'd smoked that night. He was surrounded by the thin haze of their smoke, illuminated in a blue ring around him by the blue light of the flickering TV set. He felt like he'd been waiting for a train that would never come.

He sat up straight in his chair and coughed quietly; he didn't want to wake his mum, have her appear attentively at the door with the piss jug in one hand. He shook his head to clear his thoughts and took a deep breath, filling his lungs with resolve. He wheeled himself over to the medicine cabinet. He reached out with his curled fists and plucked a brown prescription bottle of sleeping pills from the shelf.

Wedging the bottle between the backs of his hands, he jammed the cap into his mouth. Using his tongue as a wedge he pressed and turned the lid, and the child-proof cap popped easily. Charlie unscrewed it and spat the cap onto the ground.

He looked down into the bottle and examined the jumble of yellow pills inside. He closed his eyes and took a final deep breath. It wasn't hard to wedge the bottle in his mouth again and tip back his head to allow the pills to tumble out. The dry powdery discs hit the back of his throat and immediately he started to choke. He fell forward coughing. The bottle and the pills tumbled down his front. By the time his coughing fit subsided, his lap and the carpet were dotted with them.

Charlie looked at the mess. He brushed pills off his lap with his forearm and stared at the empty pill bottle lying on its side at his feet. Tears rolled down his cheeks as the anger of deep frustration rose in him. He cried out in the darkness and slammed his twisted fist into the wall.

22

Rix and Sherry's baby girl slept soundly, curled up in a soft pink blanket. Charlie's mum rocked the child gently in her practised arms. Charlie's dad peered silently over her shoulder at the child's wrinkled face.

"Oh, Sherry. She's so beautiful," Mrs Rowntree said, filling up. "Mustn't get too sentimental or I'll want one myself, eh?" Charlie's father grunted and slipped out of the room. She handed the tiny bundle back to Sherry. Rix sat next to her on the sofa, looking on proudly.

"Looks a little too much like Yoda to me," said Sam, perched on the window-ledge.

"She does not . . ." said Sherry.

"Yoda or not, she would have been born in that street if it weren't for you, mate," said Charlie.

"Yeah, we owe you," said Rix.

"Maybe that's the vocalist we've been looking for . . ."

"Don't push it, mate."

"Charlie, you want a hold?" said Rix.

Charlie shook his head and held up his cigarette.

"She won't bite. . ."

"I don't think that's such a good idea . . ." said Charlie's mum.

Sherry held out her daughter. "Come on, Charlie."

Charlie shrugged.

"All right," said his mum. "But you be careful." She plucked the cigarette from Charlie's hand. "I'll better take that."

"I can do it, Mum." Charlie held up his hand so she could tuck the cigarette back between his twisted fingers. He craned around behind him and turned his hand upside down so that the butt dropped neatly into an ashtray which rested on the end of his bed. Triumphantly he turned back and held out his arms to receive the child. He took her awkwardly, cradling her stiffly by locking his hands under his armpits. "She's so light," he said, amazed.

"Seven and a half pounds," said Sherry. "Not so small when you're giving birth, I can tell you."

"Be careful, darling, she's very fragile," his mum warned.

Charlie ignored her. He bent low over the child, cooing and muttering to her as she slept. He looked up at Rix and beamed. "Best thing you ever did."

Rix nodded. The baby gave a little cough and its hands waggled free of the blankets. Charlie's mum swooped down and lifted the child from his arms.

"Gently does it . . ." She handed the baby back to Sherry. Charlie glowered at his mother. "She's tired, darling," she said defensively.

"Yeah, maybe we should be going," said Rix.

Charlie slumped in his chair, sulking. Sherry, Sam and Rix stood up to go.

"Well, thanks for coming. It cheers Charlie up no end. Doesn't it, love?"

Charlie shook his head in disbelief. Rix clapped him on the shoulder.

"Glad . . . to . . . be . . . of . . . some . . . assistance," he said slowly and loudly, as if Charlie was deaf. Charlie chuckled.

"See you soon, Uncle Charlie," said Sherry as she kissed him.

Sam feigned ducking away from Charlie's mum and waved. "Later."

"Later, mate."

Charlie's mum followed them out. Alone in his room, Charlie wheeled himself across to the window. He pulled back the net curtains to watch his friends leave. They kissed each other and chatted, making plans for the coming week. Sherry held the baby close to her, pushing the blanket away from its tiny face with her finger.

Charlie smiled. Rix and Sherry were parents; who would have guessed it?

The harsh acrylic smell of burning plastic made him smart. Turning on the spot, he saw a slim column of smoke rising from his bed.

"Fuck!" With one thrust of his wheels he pulled up by the

bed. His ashtray had overturned onto the counterpane; his discarded butt sat at the centre of a brown circle of charred blanket. Panicking, he shoved his thumbs into the material to try and lift the smouldering sheet. The surge of air was all the material needed to catch fire, an angry blue flame growing around the singed hole.

"Fuck, fuck!" shouted Charlie pulling his hand back sharply.

He dashed back to the window. Through its heavy double-glazing he saw his mum standing at the end of the front garden, kissing Sherry on the cheek. He called her name, shouting for help, but they could not hear him. Panic seized him, spreading across his chest like a vice. He looked around the room, desperate for something to extinguish the fire. His mum's tea towel was draped across the arm of the sofa, he made a wild lunge for it. The wheel of his chair caught the sofa at speed, catapulting him forward and onto the ground. Winded and breathing hard, he dragged himself across the floor. The toxic fumes stung his throat. Pushing himself up with one hand, he lashed at the bed from the floor with the tea towel. He saw the flames lick at the side of his bed, a heavy plume of suffocating smoke growing across the ceiling. With each stroke the towel itself smouldered more until eventually it too caught fire. Charlie threw it away from him. His mind screamed with fear, with the smoke and with heat from the fire growing above him.

"Fuck, fuck. Mum, help!" He threw his arms across his face.

He felt the heavy thump of his mum's feet as she ran from the door. With two thumps of the tea towel, the fire was out.

Charlie was still whimpering as his mother crouched beside him and slowly unfolded his arms. When he saw her there he immediately began to weep.

"Mum . . . thought I was gonna burn . . . so scared, I was so fucking scared."

His mother took him in her arms. Charlie's body jerked against her as he fought for breath between the sobs. He turned his face into her chest. "What am I gonna do? What am I gonna do?"

His mother hugged him closer and tears formed in her own eyes.

"Give it time, baby, please give it time." She ran her hand through his soft blond hair. "We both need some time . . ."

23

The silent cranes were silhouetted against the setting sun as it slid down behind the docks. Charlie cocked his head and wondered what kind of shot it would make. Rix, drunk, swung an unsteady hand towards Charlie's glass. The bottle neck connected heavily with the thick glass of his pint pot. He filled it to the brim, splashing the final drop over Charlie's lap.

"Oi, get a grip!"

"There you go, my son." Rix sat down on a wooden railway sleeper that he and Sam had dragged to the water's edge to serve as a makeshift bench. Charlie held court from his chair. Rix tipped the bottle over his own glass to collect the last drizzle. When nothing came, he peered in through the neck.

"It's dead, mate," said Sam.

"Eh?"

"It's dead," Sam said more loudly.

Rix nodded and tossed the bottle over his shoulder. It flew over the edge of the dock, spinning in the air before landing in the water with a plop.

"You some kind of litter bug?" said Charlie.

"Mate, it's hardly gonna affect this place, is it?" Rix swept his hand across the deserted docks. They sat among the salt-worn debris of deserted ships and graffiti-covered containers. Broken hunks of machinery and rotting piles of cardboard were piled haphazardly against the empty warehouses. This was their first time back at the docks since the photo shoot for the band. Things hadn't changed.

"You're a disgrace," said Sam. He reached into a plastic bag of beers and pulled out another bottle. "Don't think your missus lets you out enough." Rix fumbled with a bottle opener. "What you reckon Charlie, Rix under the thumb or what?"

"Reckon he's lucky, that's what he is." Sam's face dropped. "Better to have his woman waiting up for him than his fucking mum."

179

"Don't start all that again," slurred Rix as he flipped the tin lid off his bottle. "You got us, man . . . people who love you."

"Yeah," agreed Sam. "What if in ten years from now they can fix you up? What would we say to your mum then?"

Charlie furrowed his brow. "What you saying? Wait ten years just in case."

"No, we're saying you still got lots to live for now."

"Try sitting here and say that."

Rix was sobered by the moment. He looked away down the river, zoning out on the patterns in the water behind him.

"Hey!" said Sam suddenly.

Charlie jumped in his seat and placed one hand on his heart. "Fuck."

"Hang on a bit." Sam jumped up. "I've got something for you." He trotted over to Rix's van and pulled a parcel out of the back. He hurried back to Charlie and dropped it triumphantly in his lap.

"What's this?" Rix sat forward and eyed the box and its ornate bow.

"Open it," urged Sam.

Charlie handed his glass to Rix. He slipped the bow with one thumb and pulled at the paper. It wouldn't give; his fingers slid across its shiny surface. He looked up at Rix in exasperation.

"Hang on." Rix leant over him and tore through the paper, opening it like a flower on Charlie's lap to reveal a white box. Rix delicately slid off the lid. Inside was a cube of steel, leather and glass; a brand-new Hasselblad box camera.

"Full on!" said Rix, looking at Sam.

"Latest top bollocks that," said Sam proudly. "Professional spec." Sam sat down looking to Charlie with an eager smile.

Charlie remained silent, his head bowed. He stared long and hard at the camera but made no move to touch it. Finally he looked up and said, "What the fuck am I gonna do with this?"

Sam looked confused.

"Look at me, man. I couldn't even get the wrapper off."

Sam was hurt. "Don't have to hold it . . . when you get

your insurance through you can get an assistant to set it all up. I thought . . ."

"Thought what?" Charlie cut in. "I could do what I did? Be what I was? Give him a camera and everything's all right again?" Charlie's top lip quivered with anger.

"Charlie, he was just trying . . ." said Rix.

"You can't sit back and fade away!" said Sam.

Charlie took a deep breath. "You just don't get it, do you? The most basic things in life, the things you do without even thinking, are like *mountains* I have to climb every fucking day." Charlie shook his head bitterly. "Until I can deal with that, all this is just a fantasy."

Sam looked away crestfallen.

Rix drained the last of his bottle.

Charlie gave a grunt and twitched in his chair.

"We get the point," said Rix.

Charlie inhaled sharply with a weird rattle.

"Eh?" Rix watched him, confused.

Charlie's arms were sucked in tight against his torso as a spasm racked his body. The camera slid from his knees, pitching a divot into the earth at his feet. He grabbed both sides of his head and shouted, "Shit . . . my head!" Rix grabbed him by the shoulders. "What? What?"

Charlie's face contorted as he struggled to speak.

"What the fuck is it?"

He fought for breath, coughing as pain flashed across his skull. "Tube's blocked. My bag." He gasped.

Sam was on his feet too, wide-eyed with panic. "Oh fuck, oh fuck."

"It's his colostomy bag," said Rix.

"So?" said Sam, holding out his palms in disbelief.

Rix looked around and stuttered: "So, so. Charlie what do we do?"

"Change it!" he screamed. "Change it now."

"Get him in the van," said Rix.

They grabbed Charlie under each arm and pulled him out of his chair. They dragged him across the bumpy waste ground, his heels cutting two furrows in the earth behind them. He twisted and jerked as they laid him out on the iron floor of Rix's van. Charlie, breathing hard, frantically pushed down his trousers to expose a thin plastic tube that snaked out from his belly. The tube was taped down across his stomach and terminated in a clear plastic sack which was strapped to the inside of his leg. Sam and Rix knelt by him in the van, staring at the tube in disbelief. Charlie was flushed red, his eyes watering with agony. His voice was husky as he barked instructions at them.

"Catheter. Pull it out."

Rix fumbled in his jeans for his keys. "Let's get you home, quick! Sam you drive."

"No time," croaked Charlie. "Pull it out now!"

Sam was shaking his head. "We can't do this, Charlie. We don't know how!"

Charlie grabbed Sam's shirt front and pulled himself up. "Pull it out, Sam!"

Sam peeled back the dressing that covered the end of the tube to reveal the neat hole in Charlie's stomach it was plugged into.

"Do it!"

Sam wrinkled his nose as he pulled the warm plastic gently from the soft flesh of Charlie's belly. It seemed to go on for ever. Each inch released a pungent sulphurous stench. Sam felt his head spin. As the end of the tube popped free it spat a jet of urine across the floor of the van.

"Christ!"

"Put your thumb over the end . . . hold it up," ordered Charlie.

With the tube at arm's length, Sam untaped the bag from Charlie's thigh. Rix looked on and frowned, his mouth curled with disgust.

"Good," said Charlie.

Sam threw the bag out of the back of the van. It landed in the darkness with a squelch.

"Rix!" ordered Charlie. Rix jumped. "Find a collection bag and a fresh tube."

Rix nodded and rummaged in Charlie's box of medical supplies. Finally he produced a tube and bag. "This?"

Charlie caught his breath. He pressed the back of his hand to his forehead, riding a sharp wave of pain. "Yeah," he nodded. "Put the tube in the bag and seal it." Rix licked his lips in concentration as he sealed the two together.

"Right. Now give it to Sam."

"Oh, Jesus," said Sam under his breath. He took the tube.

"Sam, you know what to do."

Sam closed his eyes and took a deep breath. "I can't believe I'm doing this." He half covered his eyes with one hand and slid the fresh tube into the hole.

Ten minutes later, it was over. Sam and Rix sat on the edge of the van's rear door and looked into the gloom. Both of them were in deep shock. Rix was absently counting the lights on Canary Wharf tower. Sam stared in horror at Charlie's discarded colostomy bag, which had landed a few feet from them like some pissy jellyfish. Charlie still lay flat out in the van, his feet twitching between them like glove puppets. With the blockage removed, the poison cleared from his bloodstream and the pain subsided. An air of terrible embarrassment fell on them. Lying on the van's dusty floor, Charlie stared at the yellow tin of Rix's roof and wondered what to do. He propped himself up on his elbows and looked at the hunched rounds of their backs. They were clearly traumatised. They'd also been good enough mates to stand by him when it counted.

"So, darlings," he asked. "Was it good for you, too?"

They turned to face him. Something about their haunted eyes cracked him up. Charlie sniggered. Then he started to laugh.

"Fucking hell!" muttered Sam, suppressing a smile.

The laughter built in him too. Finally Rix lost it, shaking so hard he fell down next to Charlie. Sam followed suit. The three of them rolled on their backs, their laughter echoing around the tiny cab of the van.

Bean took a final drag on his cigarette, pulling the ash in a glowing ring right down to the filter. He dropped the butt onto the ground and crushed it with the toe of his trainer. He coughed and leant back against the concrete pillar he hid behind, tucking his stiff white hands under his arms for warmth. He heard the curt beep of a car horn and ducked his head around the pillar to see if it was business. A huge Mercedes stood on the kerb, its exhaust fumes frozen in a grey cloud with the chill afternoon air. He knew the Mercedes was Ricky's, there was no other car like it on the estate. The car had none of the wide-boy trimmings of Elroy's. It was a sleek black machine, showroom fresh and top of the range. The engine was so quiet that Bean hadn't even noticed it slide to a halt next to him. One of its shiny windows slid down to reveal Ricky relaxing over its dark leather seats. He grinned broadly. Without a word he beckoned Bean over.

Bean was confused, as Ricky seldom came down to the front line, least of all to see him; but knew better than to hang around. He quickly checked the road was clear and then trotted over.

"All right, Ricky," he said, rubbing his hands together against the cold. He peered into the car and saw Blondie at the wheel.

"Am I disturbin' something?" asked Ricky.

"Nah, I'm nearly finished for the day."

Ricky looked Bean up and down. "You been selling a fair bit for me, Bean?" he said.

Bean nodded. "A fair bit."

"I like that." Ricky laughed. "That's cool, *real* cool."

Bean gave a nervous grin. "Thank you."

Ricky's face hardened. He pinched the bridge of his nose. "I know you been raisin' your price to cover your smoke."

Bean was shocked. "Ricky, I ain't . . ."

Ricky held up a hand to silence him. He adjusted the tight knot of his tie. "I don't mind this. You may be white but you ain't stupid. Just make sure you pay me for what you take."

"But . . ." Bean pleaded.

"You the man now, Bean. Me sort you out, *direct,* no problem." Ricky leaned towards the window. He cast a slow critical eye over Bean's dirty designer sports clothes and super-baggy trousers. "Get yourself cleaned up and come down to me club. Bring that bloodclat Elroy."

"Ricky, I . . ."

"Tonight," he said finally. "Maybe we make this a white Christmas after all." Ricky backed it up with a threatening smile. Bean knew it was bad news, Ricky never came to the estate unless he had to. Resigning himself, he grunted a yes. Ricky slapped his hand on the back of the headrest in front of him. "Go-wan!" he said to Blondie.

As the big car purred away, Bean wondered what the hell he had got himself into.

24

The lights went down plunging the venue into darkness. Shouts and whistles broke from the crowd as they jostled to get a better view. Dry-ice machines hissed and a great white frozen cloud drifted across the stage. Colour spotlights darted in the mist. Almost imperceptibly at first, a flat synthesised heartbeat grew from the speakers slowly engulfing the crowd. The atmosphere became heavier, until it was as thick as soup. From behind the fog came Rix's sounds of the city, sweeping like a dream from one side of the stage to another. A single bright white beam cut down from the roof to plant a smoking silver disc in the centre of the stage. There was a pause then Iona stepped into it from the darkness. Her hair was piled high on her head and she wore tight fluorescent clothing; ribbons hung from her arms and legs. In the sharp spotlight she looked almost robotic, her faced chiselled, top-lit and demonic. She raised her microphone and sang, filling the hall with a sweet haunting diva's song that floated across the heads of people. As her harmony grew, a single perfect note dropped down behind her voice like a bomb. When it hit home so did Rix.

In a blaze of flashing light, the beats came alive. Rix was set up on a platform behind Iona hunched over a bank of synthesisers, bouncing wildly to the music. The crowd went wild, roaring their approval. Rix held one arm aloft and, with a flick of his wrist, cued the other musicians, a bass player on one side of the stage, a drummer on the other. The music was pumped, gelled and then started rocking the place.

Charlie sat up in the balcony dancing in his chair and slapping his palms on its arms in time to the beat. After Rix, he probably knew this song better than anyone else in the world and this was just how he'd imagined G.M.T. live. Wild, tribal and totally engulfing. He cupped his hands round his mouth and shouted encouragement down towards the stage. Not that Rix needed it. The crowd was a seething mass of jumping bodies. The crazy animations of their projected backdrop were tattooed across Rix's face. Charlie could see his friend totally absorbed as he pored over the knobs and dials of his equipment. But this time there was something different. His customary sombre grimace was gone; instead he was grinning like a maniac. Rix was getting it all right, the best feeling in the world.

Charlie felt a tap on his shoulder. It was Sam, leaning precariously across the rope that separated the reserved area from the rest of the crowd. He was holding out a pint of lager.

"Here you go . . ." he shouted.

Charlie shoved his thumb through the glass handle and took the pint pot. "Cheers!" Charlie nodded towards the stage. "Fucking excellent, mate!"

Sam grinned. For once in his life he looked self-effacing. "Yeah, they're kicking it. You all right? I mean, got everything you need?"

Charlie knocked back a slug of beer and wiped off his mouth with the back of his gloved hand. "Don't worry about me. Go do your manager bit."

"Sure?"

Charlie ducked his chin down onto his chest and he let out a burp. He gave Sam a sloppy grin.

"I guess that means yes. Okay, back in a minute."

Sam pushed into the crowd. He slid between pint glasses and under cigarettes until he got to the stairwell. He looked over at the stage again. The opening number climaxed; the stage went dark again with Iona frozen in the spotlight. The roof nearly came off the place. Iona staggered back across the stage, her face glistening with sweat, unable to believe the reception. She gave a coy bow. "Take it easy," she said with a laugh. "We're just the opening act!"

She wiped her face on a towel. The flat beats of tabla ushered in the next song. Sam saw Iona catch Rix's eye across his keyboard and point at him, a little sign of respect. Rix gave a chuckle, his face hidden coyly under his dreads. Iona turned back to the crowd.

"We're called G.M.T. And this is our first gig!"

The noise was deafening, the crowd cheered and clapped; some even stamped on the floor demanding more.

Sam jogged down the stairs and, patting the bouncer on the shoulder, he ducked into the VIP bar. He scanned the crowded room, looking for his guests. A hand grabbed him by the elbow and spun him round. It was Henry, dressed for the occasion in blue silk. He engulfed Sam in a huge bear hug.

"Your dad would be so proud of you." Henry stepped back and slapped him hard on the back. "And I am too, darling."

"Thanks, that means a lot." Sam smiled and walked on into the bar.

"Sam," called Sherry. She stood by a corner table with Bobby and her mystery woman, Deborah.

Sam gave a wave and wandered over to join them. He kissed Sherry on both cheeks and then turned to Bobby. "I'm really pleased you made it."

Bobby was satisfied that he was sincere and patted him on the elbow. "Well done, Sam. You finally pulled it off."

Sam nodded towards the door that led to the stage. "Still part of you out there, Bob."

Bobby blushed. "Yeah."

"Sam," said Sherry. "Have you met Deborah?"

Sam turned to Bobby's girlfriend. "Not properly, no." He held out his hand. "Hi, Sam Jackson."

Deborah took his hand and shook it firmly. "Hello, Sam. Deborah Shaw. Heard all about you."

Sam looked back at Bobby and raised an eyebrow. "I'll bet you have."

"Hello, Sam," said a voice behind him.

Sam turned to see Rachel. She carried four brimming drinks.

"Thanks for the ticket."

Sam was speechless. He looked at Rachel for a second, trying to compose himself. "You came. I mean . . ." he tripped over the words.

"Think I'd miss this?" Rachel handed out drinks to the girls.

Sam leaned closer to her. "Look, Rachel, we need to talk."

"Not tonight," she said firmly.

"Fine, tomorrow then."

Rachel shook her head and took a sip of her pint. "Some things never change."

"That's where you're wrong," said Sam. "Let me take you for lunch tomorrow. No strings." Out of the corner of his eye, Sam saw Henry waving at him wildly from the other side of the room. "Look, I've gotta go."

Rachel shrugged as Sam moved off.

"Once bitten twice shy, eh, Rachel?" said Sherry.

"Oh, fuck off," she said, laughing. "Come on! Let's see if this boyfriend of yours is all he's cracked up to be."

Charlie grooved away, quite indifferent to the crowd around him. He took another enthusiastic swig from his pint and wiped his mouth with the back of his hand. It gave him an idea. He formed a rough circle with his thumb and forefinger and stuffed it in his mouth. Even he was impressed with the whistle he pulled off. He laughed at the achievement and then whistled again, this time even louder.

A dark figure ducked under the rope and sat down next to him. Without taking his eyes from the stage Charlie said, "Sorry, mate, that seat's taken." He gave another whistle, trying to get in time with the beat.

"Hello, Charlie," said the figure.

Charlie swung round to see Bean, his glazed eyes fixed on the stage, a woollen beanie hat pulled down low across his forehead. Despite the heat in the hall he wore a hooded top and huge Puffa jacket.

"Fuck, Bean! Come here, let me take a look at you!"

Bean didn't shift.

"Don't know what all the fuss is. Her tits ain't no bigger than mine, bredren . . ." He gave a dirty laugh.

"Should be you up there, Bean . . ." said Charlie.

Bean turned on him sharply, his face softening into a smile. "What? Nah, mate, not me. No regrets . . ."

"Where you been, man?" continued Charlie.

Bean was not paying attention. Across the heads of the

crowd, he saw Sherry and Bobby emerge from the bar. Behind them was Rachel. Bean felt his chest seize with panic, he couldn't face her. He got quickly to his feet and grabbed the back of Charlie's chair.

"What you doing?"

He ducked out of the girls' view and whispered in Charlie's ear. "C'mon, mate, let's get some air."

Bean kicked open a fire door and wheeled Charlie out onto the wrought-iron platform which was screwed to the top of the fire escape. A plume of steam followed them out of the baking venue, escaping into the winter cold. He flicked on the brake again and swung round in front of Charlie, leaning casually back against the handrail.

"You all right, then?" asked Charlie.

The dark bags under Bean's eyes and his pasty skin answered for him.

"Sure, course I am! On top of the fuckin' world, geezer . . ." He gestured as he spoke with a jerky amphetamine twitch.

"Just that you looked fucked!"

The blistered dry skin around Bean's mouth cracked as he smiled "I was fucked the day my dad shot his load . . . mate." Bean grinned again. "Funny, ain't it? How it all comes down to whose dick you was launched from . . ." Charlie shrugged. Bean leant down towards him. "But we're out there now, man. Me and you . . . stared death in the fucking face." Bean pointed into the hall. "All those other wankers don't have a clue . . ."

"I didn't stare death in the face. I stared life in the face," said Charlie. "Death is an absolute. There's nothing absolute about life . . . Any time you want out, door's always open . . ."

Bean's bravado crumbled and he sat down at Charlie's feet.

"For a long time, mate, I wasn't sure which I wanted more." Bean looked at him again and for a second Charlie saw him as he had on their very first day of primary school. Little Bean, the new kid; frightened, damaged and unloved.

"You're still the man, Charlie," he said quietly. "When we was kids, you made my cunt life better. Wanted to thank you . . ."

Sam's voiced echoed from the hall behind them.

"Charlie?" He burst out onto the fire escape. "Charlie! You all right? What you doing out here?" Charlie held out his hand to stop Sam in his tracks. "What's going on?" asked Sam.

"Nothing," said Charlie. "Just getting some air."

"Well, let's get back in, eh? I don't want my guest of honour freezing to death."

As Sam wheeled him backwards through the door, Charlie caught a final glimpse of Bean disappearing like a ghost into the night.

Elroy's car was waiting in the alley that ran down the side of the venue. The courtesy light flashed on as Bean opened his door to reveal Elroy sitting behind the wheel. He was chopping out two lines of cocaine on a CD cover.

"You get the money off that geezer?" he asked.

Bean sat down next to him. "Nah. He just left."

Elroy snorted up a line noisily through a rolled-up banknote. He offered the CD cover to Bean. Bean shook his head.

"We straight with Ricky now?" asked Bean.

Elroy snorted up the other line. "Yeah, man," Elroy said. He wiped the cover with his fingers and rubbed the last few crumbs across his gums.

"You sure?"

Elroy looked at him. "Yeah!" he said defensively.

"Then why we gotta go down there? Let's just go home."

Elroy sighed. "Because he wants to see us. And if Ricky says he wants to see you, you go. Right?"

Bean lit a cigarette. He wound down the window to toss out a spent match.

"I don't like it."

"Tough." Elroy started the engine. "Just chill out. It's just a friendly visit, yeah."

Bean doubted there was anything friendly about Ricky.

25

Ricky's club was a converted warehouse down by Deptford docks, a squat concrete bunker on the edge of an industrial estate. Posters advertising ragga records and house music peeled off its tiled walls. The windows had been blacked out and fortified with steel mesh. No one went down to the docks at night, not even the police, so from midnight to sunrise the club and the roads and alleys around it, belonged to Ricky.

Elroy and Bean cruised past the queue: a scruffy-looking mix of rastas, ravers and local lowlife. The queue ran down one side of the building and terminated under a fizzing neon sign which bore the club's name, Paradise. Bouncers in dinner jackets stood in front of its heavy steel doors, arms folded and sunglasses on despite the darkness. Their admission policy was entirely random. They simply dragged punters from the queue on a whim and shoved them across the threshold of the club. A second group of bouncers waited inside to run a metal detector over their customers to divest them of guns and knives.

Bean and Elroy parked up. They walked across to the head of the queue with their best gangsta strut.

Elroy caught a bouncer's eye.

"Here to see Ricky, bro."

The bouncer nodded and pushed a couple of rastas out of the doorway to clear a path for them. They walked past security and into the black interior of the club. It was dark and thunderously loud. Hard ragga shook the windowpanes in their frames. On stage an MC was toasting to the music, a heavy Jamaican refrain so fast it was indecipherable.

As they pushed through the crowd those who recognised Elroy and Bean stood back in respect. Those who didn't felt the bouncer's hands on their chest and cheeks cannoning them back into the crowd, spilling drinks and knocking joints and cigarettes flying.

A second steel door was buried deep at the back of the club.

A sign on the door read 'Private'. Not that it mattered, you would have needed dynamite to get it open. The bouncer rapped on it with the fat knuckle of his muscular fist. A peephole slid open in the metal and a pair of eyes looked out. Heavy bolts were pulled back behind the door and it swung open. Ricky's bodyguard, Blondie, filled the doorway. He stood with his coat open, one hand rested on the pistol stuck in his belt. He nodded the pair in and slammed the door behind him.

Ricky's office was quiet, sparsely furnished and lit with a warm red light. A big grey safe dominated one wall. Its thick door hung open; inside were neat stacks of used notes bound with rubber bands and a pair of automatic pistols. Bean's eyes widened. There had to be a couple of hundred grand there. A banker's automatic counting machine sat on top of the safe next to an accountant's ledger. On the floor there was a sports bag still half full of cash. They had disturbed Ricky doing his accounts.

Ricky sat at the far end of the room at an enormous wooden partner's desk. Behind him a huge framed map of Jamaica covered the wall. Engrossed in making some drinks, there was a dusty bottle of over-proof rum at his elbow along with a cocktail ice box. His brow was knotted with concentration as he crushed the juice from a lime with a small pocket knife.

Blondie nudged Bean and Elroy in the back, silently directing them towards a couple of fat leather armchairs in front of the desk. Blondie took up position behind them, arms folded across his chest. Ricky ground at the lime until he was satisfied it could give no more. He flicked the juice off his hands and he dried himself with a napkin.

He looked at them over the desk, his face half in shadow from the desk lamp. Then he scooped a fist full of ice from the box and dropped a few cubes into each of the three glasses that sat in front of him. He poured a generous measure of the rum into the first glass. He held it up and admired his work, turning the glass in the lamp light.

"Me father give me 'dis drink when he think I become a

man," he announced. "When we got drunk, then 'im try to beat me." He raised his glass to Bean in a toast and tipped it back in one shot. Ricky smacked his lips and inverted the empty glass, placing it deliberately back on the table. "But 'im lost because I was a man." Picking up the bottle, he poured measures into the remaining two glasses. "As a man, me 'ave a reputation. An' me is gonna keep that reputation . . . *solid*." Ricky stared at Bean. "You understand?"

Bean shifted uneasily in his seat. "Yeah, course, Ricky, man, I understand . . ."

Blondie stepped forward and lifted the remaining two drinks off the desk. He handed one glass to Bean and the other to Elroy. Bean returned the toast to Ricky and took a gulp. He coughed as the powerful spirit bit into his throat.

"Was the matter? Don't like the taste?" Ricky was grinning. "A little bit too strong, maybe?"

Bean winced and finished his drink. "Gotta get used to it," he croaked. "Acquired taste."

Blondie took Bean's empty glass and stepped back into the shadows.

"Just like you acquired a taste for my money . . ." he spat.

Bean was puzzled. "What?"

"Me tell you, raisin' the price for your smoke is cool. But you pay for what you take!"

Bean realised he was in big trouble, he looked at Elroy hoping for some explanation. "Fuck is this?"

Ricky slammed his fists onto his desk.

"Where's ma fuckin' money, bitch?"

Bean stood up and looked around wildly. "This is bullshit." He looked again at Elroy, who had his eyes down, hiding from Bean's glare under his palms.

"I never took nuffin," pleaded Bean.

"There's no point lying, Bean," said Elroy calmly.

Bean stared at his friend as the penny finally dropped. Elroy's new car, his fancy wardrobe. They had cost a lot more than the two of them made. Elroy had creamed it off the top and set Bean up to take the wrap. "You fucking bastard!"

Before Bean could lunge at Elroy, Blondie grabbed him

from behind, driving the cold steel muzzle of his pistol into Bean's neck.

"Where's the money, weird cunt?" he hissed.

Bean froze. Chilled with calm built of pure rage, he turned to face Ricky. He spoke in a clear, level voice. "I never took nothing from you."

Ricky's eyes were blazing. No white boy stole from him and no white boy was going to look at him without even breaking a sweat.

"What me do?" asked Blondie.

"Shoot 'im in the kneecap . . ."

Blondie pulled back the hammer on his pistol with a click.

Elroy leapt to his feet, his eyes bulging with adrenalin. "Shoot the cunt!"

Bean grabbed Blondie's arm and swung himself round, rolling the big man's bulky torso across his shoulder. They wrestled together in a tight huddle until a muffled shot broke between them. Blondie spun away from Bean, blood pumped from a wound in his stomach.

Blondie fell backwards, his body shaking with shock. Spasms in his hand pulled the trigger on his gun. The first shot tore a hole in Ricky's map of Jamaica. As he hit the ground his gun fired again, the bullet went clean through Ricky's skull. Ricky died instantly, falling into his chair like a ragdoll. His head hit the desk with a thump, a pool of dark blood spreading between the lime rinds.

"Oh fuck!" said Elroy, surveying the carnage. He looked across at Bean.

Bean stood motionless, looking back at Elroy, his eyes blank with shock. In his hand was the gun Elroy had bought, wisps of smoke escaping from its barrel.

Elroy laughed nervously. "Thank fuck you remembered to bring that. We really sorted those cunts out."

Bean raised the gun and looked along its barrel at Elroy. "Tools of the trade, you lying piece of shit."

Elroy shook. His voice broke as he choked on tears. "Oh, Christ! Oh, shit. Please, Bean, no . . ." He backed away from Bean.

"Death is an absolute. Any time you want out, door's always open."

Elroy stopped. He sniffed back his tears. "Yeah, yeah. I got it . . ." He clasped and unclasped his hands in a desperate effort to remember. "Wait a minute . . . American film, yeah?"

Bean fired three rounds into his gut. Elroy folded and fell to the ground with a gurgle; he twitched once and then he was gone.

Bean felt strangely calm as he looked around the remains of the office. The muffled thumps of the music breathed through the walls like a heartbeat. He studied his reflection in the cracked glass of Ricky's Jamaica map. There was a single speck of blood on his cheek. He wiped it off with his thumb and tucked the pistol back into his waistband.

"All good things must come to an end," he said quietly.

He went across to the safe and picked up the sports bag, worked fast, stuffing it with cash.

Bean had been in and out of Ricky's club in twenty minutes. Smooth like a magician, as the late Elroy would have said. He packed up the bag then leisurely washed his face in a sink in Ricky's office, slicking back his hair flat against his skull. Nobody even looked at him as he left; that was Ricky's way, in his line of work it was dangerous to ask questions.

Elroy's car had started first time. Bean wasn't stupid, picking the keys off Elroy's corpse was the first thing he'd done. Though Bean had no licence, the car was an automatic and Elroy had let him practice around the estate in his more generous moods. It was just like driving a dodgem and, after having committed a triple homicide, Bean reckoned the DVLC was the least of his worries.

He drove straight back to the flat, the sports bag on the seat next to him. How many people would be shedding tears for Ricky, or Elroy for that matter? Bean couldn't think of any but it seemed like a good idea to get out of town for a while; prison was not an option.

He had no trouble going through Elroy's flat. The place was no more home to him than his dad's had been, so Bean had no regrets leaving and there wasn't much he needed to take. A shirt of Elroy's he'd had his eye on, a couple of CDs and his trumpet. He pocketed half a dozen wraps of coke but left the rock; that was something he wouldn't need in his new life.

He drove east away from the city and up into the marshes, following a B road out into the darkness. He parked up in a lay-by and let his head clear in the silence. He wrapped his coat around him and stared out over the vast emptiness of the mud plane.

The last twelve hours had been a revelation. He'd stopped running and faced the cunts down for the first time in his life. It felt good and he wasn't going to stop now. Fate had dealt him a hand tonight and he wanted to pull together all the loose ends before he got out of this place. First to Ireland and then, who knows?

Bean contemplated the flickering lights of a distant refinery and thought about Rachel. He knew he needed her to make his life complete. And he knew she wanted him. He could remember everything about that day they spent together.

All it took was the guts to go and ask her.

26

Charlie was momentarily blinded by the flood of sunlight into his bedroom. His mother's cheery voice followed it.

"Morning, Charlie, time to get up."

He grunted and hit the button to raise the back of his bed. The electric motor whirred, propping him upright enough to have a decent cough.

"You all right, love?" asked his mum as she fastened the curtains.

Charlie chuckled. "My first hangover since Stoke Mandeville."

His mother muttered disapprovingly and wandered out. Charlie swivelled round to get the bottle of water he kept by his bed; in its place was the Hasselblad camera, out of its box and loaded with film. He must have got it out the night before; he was obviously more pissed than he'd thought. He reached across and pulled open the cupboard in the night stand to put the camera away. He stopped as he felt its familiar weight. Even in his twisted hands the camera felt strangely natural. He sat it in his lap and ran his fingers across the bumpy leather that covered most of its surface. He studied its dials and traced the shape of the lens, blinking at his own reflection in the glass.

A chill passed over him. A flashback from his previous life. He dropped the camera like it had given him an electric shock. He was frightened of everything it stood for.

Leaning back against the pillows, he looked at the wall of his pictures. There was Henry's party on the *Cutty Sark*, an antiracism march through Brixton, the terraces at the football; all the images of his youth, full of movement and life. In pride of place was the band photo for G.M.T.: Rix, Bobby and Bean in a moody montage down the docks. They looked so young, fresh-faced like school kids, radiating optimism and naivety.

Charlie smiled, remembering last night's gig. It had been

good, really good. And the best thing of all was that his mates had done it. The proof that they really could do anything they wanted. Stare the world in the face and tell it to go fuck itself.

Charlie looked down again at the camera in his lap. Slowly he positioned it. Through the viewfinder in its top he saw his room with a photographer's eye, framed in 20 x 20. He shifted the camera slightly to take in a beam of morning light then moved across the carpet to focus on his discarded trainers lying like two lazy lions by his bed. Finally he zoomed in on a cup of pencils on his chest of drawers, a simple still life.

Without thinking, he lifted the shutter control cable and popped the release button into his mouth. He concentrated on moving the cable into position, controlling it with his tongue. As he did he twisted the lens until the focus on the cup was just right. With a flick of his tongue the shutter clicked.

Charlie lay back and nodded with satisfaction. Great pictures.

The bedroom door swung open and his mum blustered in carrying a wooden tray stacked up with Charlie's breakfast. She stopped short at the door, puzzled by both the camera and the cable hanging out of the side of her son's mouth.

"Charlie!" she said. "What are you up to?"

Charlie chuckled and rolled the release button across his bottom lip. "Say cheese, Mum."

Rachel had a hangover that morning, too. After the gig she had gone back to Bobby's house and drunk tequila until two in the morning. Most of the conversation had been bitching about Sam, of course, but a girl needed to get that stuff off her chest every now and again. Besides, Rachel wanted to know if there really was a human being under all that bravado.

The hangover was the least of her problems. It was only eleven o'clock and the building society was already packed; each customer seemed to be ruder than the last, like some sort of nightmare consumer competition. Mr Finch had been giving her the eye all morning; he didn't like his girls 'worse for wear' on the society's time.

'No excitement,' Rachel thought to herself. 'Just keep your head down until five and then you're out of here.'

27

Sam was on a high. Last night's gig had created some serious interest in the band. The phone hadn't stopped ringing all morning. Journalists, producers and record company A&R men all wanted a piece of the action. G.M.T. were going to be big. They were going to be huge.

By twelve he'd had enough. He decided to celebrate by taking Rachel out for a slap-up meal. This was the chance he needed to sort things out. 'I love you': who would have thought that Sam Jackson would ever say that and mean it?

He gave his secretary a vague excuse about meeting clients and took a cab down to the high street. The cab dropped him off right outside Rachel's building society. Sam paid the driver generously and went to go in. Then he thought better of it. Even he could see that in the light of recent events a bit of tact might be in order. He remembered there was always a flower stall set up outside the railway station. It was a beautiful spring morning and he was in no hurry. He'd surprise her with a huge bunch of flowers and beg her for a chance at a fresh start.

Supremely pleased with himself, Sam wandered down the high street, hands in pockets, whistling as he went.

Behind him a mud-stained white Mercedes drove across the double yellow line and bumped up onto the kerb.

Bean wrenched on the handbrake and killed the engine. He bent over a CD cover and came up sniffing. Grabbing the sports bag from the seat next to him, he opened the door and stepped purposefully out.

The building society was packed with the lunch-time rush. Neat queues had formed in front of the tills; rows of everyday folk impatiently holding chequebooks and sacks of change. Bean pushed the glass doors open with a flourish. He strode in, swinging the sports bag by his side. He moved along the back wall, examining each snaking queue, jumping up on tiptoes to snatch a look at the cashier behind the glass. Three cubicles from the door he saw Rachel. He shoved his way to front of the queue and planted the bag on the till in front of her.

Rachel was counting out money for an elderly gentlemen.

"There's a queue, young man," he said as Bean crushed in next to him.

"Whatever."

Rachel finished counting the money. She tapped the notes gently on her desktop and dropped them into the metal delivery drawer.

"Thank you, sir."

Bean loomed into view on the other side of the glass; Rachel's mouth dropped open with shock.

"Bean! Jesus! What you doing here?"

Bean smiled broadly revealing an uneven row of yellow, stained teeth.

"You look well, Rachel."

"You look like . . . shit," she said.

He did. His skin was grey and the sores around his mouth were an angry red in the daylight; his sleepless eyes were bloodshot and his nose drizzled from Elroy's badly cut cocaine.

Bean shrugged and continued in his suavest voice. "Thank you." He was transfixed. Rachel was more beautiful than he'd remembered. "So, Ireland," he said. He unzipped the bag and pulled it apart so Rachel could see the pile of wadded notes inside.

"Christ!" Rachel looked over her shoulder at Mr Finch, who was monitoring their exchange suspiciously.

"I've come into a bit of money."

"Keep your voice down," she whispered.

"It's the most beautiful place in the world," said Bean, bubbling with enthusiasm.

"What?"

"Ireland," said Bean, wild-eyed. "Still wanna go?"

Mr Finch moved quickly over to Rachel's shoulder. "Everything okay, Rachel?" he said, placing a protective arm across her chair.

Bean's face dropped.

"Fine, Mr Finch . . . he's a friend."

"A real good friend, so why don't you run along, Mr Finch," he spat.

Rachel rolled her eyes in exasperation. As she did a flash of orange caught her eye. A huge bunch of brightly coloured flowers. Sam was holding them as he marched in through the doors.

"There are people waiting. Please make your transaction and leave . . ." said Mr Finch.

Bean glared at him, furious. "I want to open an account," he said. "What you got?"

Rachel looked at Mr Finch, who nodded for her to continue. Rachel sighed and started her practised sales pitch. "We have three kinds of saver accounts for new customers: Bronze requires a minimum of one hundred pounds; Silver, five thousand and Gold twenty-five thousand."

Sam barged through the queue until he stood directly behind Bean. He held up the flowers and waved. He mouthed the words "Lunch. Now."

"This enough?" asked Bean. He slapped a fat wad of notes onto the counter.

Rachel tried to shake her head at Sam, who looked confused and put his hands together in a mock begging position.

"Nah, fuck it . . ." Bean continued. He took out another bundle. "What's that? Forty grand? Yeah . . ."

"Susan, call the police," said Mr Finch.

Bean's face hardened, his mouth shrunk to a tight mean slit. "I don't think so." He pulled the gun out from his trousers and held it above his head. He fired a single deafening shot into the roof. "You fucking want it," he shouted, scattering the screaming customers around him. They rushed towards the door. Mr Finch calmly reached under the table and hit the panic button.

"Bean, put down the gun . . ." said Rachel.

Bean sniffed. "Get out of here, Rachel. Now!" he ordered. He then spun around to find himself face to face with Sam. Suddenly he felt sick, the victim of another cruel joke. His second set-up of the day. "What you doing here, Sam?"

Sam smiled and shrugged. "Bean, come on, geezer . . . don't do this."

Rachel ran around the side of the glass wall and let herself out through the staff door. Bean was already nose to nose with Sam, flowers and all. She saw the rage grow in him again.

"What the fuck!" he screamed. "What the fuck is going on?" Bean looked at Rachel for a long empty minute, and she could see the pain of realisation crushing him from the inside. "Bean," she said.

"No."

Outside there was the noise of approaching sirens.

"Come on, Bean, let's get out of here," said Sam.

Bean raised the gun and jammed it under Sam's chin. "You ain't going nowhere, Sam . . ." He gestured towards Rachel with its barrel. "Look at her."

"Put the gun down, Bean, please," pleaded Rachel.

Sam dropped the flowers and held his hands up in defence, his face was rigid with fear.

"Fuck's sake, look at her!" Bean slammed the butt of the gun into Sam's face. Sam fell back onto the floor, blood gushing from his nose.

"Stop it, Bean! Stop it!"

Bean planted one knee onto Sam's chest and pressed the gun barrel against his cheek. "Did you fuck her?" he hissed. Sam was silent. He looked at Rachel. "Did you fuck Rachel? Yes or no!"

Sam shut his eyes and resigned himself. "Yes."

Bean's shoulders dropped and he let out a low moan as if his very spirit was crumbling. His mouth vibrated with anger, his lips struggled to hold back tears.

"Why do you hate me so much, Sam? We was supposed to be mates."

"I never hated you," said Sam.

"It wasn't like that," said Rachel. "Please, Bean . . . I can explain . . ."

"I'm done talking. You get out!" Bean pointed the gun at her.

Rachel stole a glance out of the window. Armed police were everywhere, crouched behind parked cars and rubbish bins, heavy black machine guns slung across their chests. She shook her head.

"Can't."

"Go, Rachel!" said Sam.

"Won't."

Bean was shaking his head, trying to comprehend what was happening to him.

"You had every fucking thing, and you still treated me like a cunt."

"I was jealous. You had talent, something real. All I had was money."

Bean laughed. "Jealous? Of me?"

"It's the truth," said Sam.

Bean chuckled. Stepping back from Sam, he drew himself up to his full height and cocked the gun. "Should've told me, mate, we could've swapped." He swung the gun and aimed it at Sam's head. His body shook with effort as he fought with himself to pull the trigger. He couldn't. He dropped the pistol in Sam's lap and headed for the door.

"Don't leave, Bean. Please don't go out there," said Rachel.

"You're lucky. Charlie needs you, Sam." Bean looked out through the glass door of the building society. He saw the armed police, like fat bluebottles in their flak jackets, crouching in position, watching him through their telescopic sights, fingers on the trigger.

"Bean! Please. For fuck's sake," said Sam.

Bean turned to face him one final time: "I've seen things you little people wouldn't believe. Attack ships on fire off the shoulder of Orion . . . remember, Sam?"

Sam nodded.

"All those moments lost, like tears in rain."

"Bean!"

"Time to die."

Bean walked out into the afternoon sunshine, oblivious to the shouted warnings from the police. He turned his head up to the sun, felt it warm his cheeks and soothe his salty eyes.

Against the blue of the spring sky birds swooped and dived. Bean watched them, then all of a sudden he heard his music. He heard his music in their flight, rising and falling on the wind, a feeling he had not had in years. The music swelled inside him and carried him up above the city and this life and into the perfect ether of beautiful melodies. He closed his eyes and held out his arms to embrace the music. Conducting the celestial orchestra for a final brilliant time.

There was a crack like a broken twig and Bean was dead before he hit the ground. His broken body, stained red with blood, collapsed onto the steps of the building society like a discarded ragdoll. In his face showed peace at last, his final smile.

28

IRELAND

It was funny to see Bean's dad cry. He wasn't exactly known for being the world's most sensitive man. But as the wind rushed over the sea and pulled at his yellow nicotine-stained hair they knew he was crying real tears. None of them had really expected him to come all the way over to Ireland but he had. He had turned up at the appointed time and lifted the urn containing Bean's ashes out of the boot of his car. Maybe it was just remorse at seeing another member of his family interred there; first his wife and then his son. His violence was the primary factor in both of them being there. That and the tower blocks. They'd worn the pair of them down to nothing until finally they'd just disappeared. The urn containing Bean's ashes shook in his unsteady hands. They stood and watched as his shoulders rose and fell with each sob.

Rix had his young daughter cradled in his arms. Sherry and Bobby were a few feet back, arms around each other, passing a hanky between them. Sam, grim-faced, stood by Rachel.

"Please," Bean's dad said, turning his ruddy face towards them. "I don't know what to do."

Charlie wheeled forward across the grass and took the urn from him.

"Thank you."

That was his goodbye. He turned his back on the bay and walked to his little red hire car. He started the engine and drove back up the bumpy track that led to the water's edge without looking back. The last they ever saw of him.

Charlie, holding the remains of his friend, looked around the group.

"What do we do now?" he said.

No one knew what to say, so they said nothing. He held out the urn and nodded to Sam, who slid off its lid. Charlie looked around him and waited for a crack in the clouds. A suitable moment.

"Rest in peace, geezer," he said as he tipped over the pot. "We're gonna miss you."

The first lump of ash fell out. It was caught by a sudden gust of wind and burst, sending a swollen grey cloud back towards Rachel. The cloud swirled briefly and pressed itself like a gauze blanket across the wool of her overcoat. Rachel leapt back with a squeal.

"Watch it, mate," added Rix, cupping a protective hand over his daughter's eyes.

"Sorry."

"'Sno problem." Rachel looked down at her overcoat. Bean was still clinging to her.

Sam took her gently by the elbow and brushed her down with the back of his hand. He smiled at Rachel and winked.

"Sometimes it ain't so easy to get south London off ya."

"You said it, mate," said Rix with a grin. "Come on, Charlie, get on with it."

Charlie shook the pot again to empty it. This time the ash poured freely, puffing briefly in the clear air before settling on the water. It darkened and then disappeared.

Charlie watched the water, its ever changing movement and the dazzling spots of the sun's reflection in the peaks of its black waves.

"I'm freezing," said Sherry behind him.

"Let's get back to the car," said Bobby. She looped her arm under Rachel's as she went.

"Rix?" called Sherry.

"Just a moment." Rix joined Charlie and Sam at the water's edge. "You all right, mate?"

"Yeah." Charlie paused. He looked up at Rix, baby in hand, and chuckled. "Fuck it, mate. We've come a long way."

Rix's daughter gave a gurgle and he bounced her gently in his arms.

"We took on the world, mate," said Rix.

Charlie nodded.

"And what have we become?"

"Real human beings, mate," said Sam. "Real human beings."